THE MENDOCINO
BOOK CLUB
NELLIE BROOKS

Merpaper Press LLC

ISBN-13: 978-1-958957-11-0

Published by Merpaper Press LLC

Edited by Karen Meeus Editing

CONTENTS

CHAPTER 1

"The moving truck is not going to get here today, Hannah." Evan set his phone on the car dash as he stared at the pretty seaside cottage in front of them.

Confused, Hannah unbuckled her seat belt and brushed back an unruly corkscrew curl threaded with the first strands of silver. "Was that a text from the company?"

After months of planning and arranging their move from San Jose to Mendocino Beach, she'd expected things to work smoothly. That included having the truck get to her mother's old cottage before she and her husband arrived. "They said they'd be here for sure."

"I know. I know they did." He turned to her, a wary look in his eyes. "Hannah. Sometimes, things change. Sometimes, things don't go according to plan."

"It's my forty-fifth birthday today, honey," she said cheerfully. "I'm no spring chicken. I'm well aware things don't always go according to plan. But I'm okay. You know me. I'm always okay." She smiled and, for a moment, cupped his smooth cheek in her hand, giving her husband her undivided attention.

To her, it had been a pleasant drive. But Evan's shirt was crumpled, and he looked sweaty and hot. Maybe navigating the bay area traffic had been more stressful than she'd realized. All the long drive over the mountain range, he had barely talked.

Feeling a surge of love, Hannah hummed reassuringly, caressing his cheek with her thumb.

Evan was taking the move hard; that was something else she hadn't expected. He had agreed to it readily enough when Hannah's old childhood home in Mendocino Beach had come on the market for the first time in decades. Hannah had been beyond excited to see the listing. Her heart had hammered almost painfully hard in her chest when she rushed into her husband's office, a print-out of the listing in hand.

He'd studied the listing distractedly first, then more interestedly—Hannah forever told him stories of the happy years she'd spent there as a child. His bare tolerance of her excitement had turned into questions and interest, and finally a light dawned in his eyes that told her all she wanted to know. They would have a new beginning by the sea!

The next day, Evan had called the listing agent and put down an offer; when it was accepted, they celebrated with laughter, champagne, and sushi.

But now, looking wary and disheveled, Evan frowned. His eyes roamed her face as if he was searching for something he'd lost. "Are you all right?" His voice was quiet, almost as if he was asking himself, not her.

Hannah tipped her head, not sure what had changed. Evan grew up in San Jose and loved the bustling bay area. Was he suddenly worried that Mendocino was too out of the way after all? She'd have to make sure that he was comfortable in the beginning. Luckily, he still had his frequent business trips to San Francisco. He could stay an extra week here and there, to catch up with old friends.

"Of course I am all right," she replied lightly. "Look at how beautiful it is, honey. Who cares if the truck and our things are a little late? How can I mind not having a sofa when we have all this?"

He drew back, pulling away from her.

She dropped her hand on her lap. "Maybe tonight it'll be a little annoying. But now? Just look at the sea." She turned to the view and spread her hands to make her point.

The cheerful white cottage stood on a sweeping bluff, surrounded by a sprawling garden full of blooming flowers. Beyond the garden twinkled the sparkling Pacific Ocean, with sandy paths running down the bluff to the famous beach that gave the small town its name.

"Smell that, honey?" She closed her eyes and inhaled deeply. The sea breeze streaming through Hannah's open window was sweetly fragrant with the scent of honeysuckle and roses, beach daisies and lavender. But best of all was the wild undercurrent of salt and seaweed, of wide-open blue water and golden sand, of crashing waves and screaming gulls, of foggy mornings and sunbaked afternoons.

"It's gorgeous," he admitted absentmindedly.

Hannah was itching to get out of the car. But her husband clearly needed a moment. "It really is gorgeous," she encouraged him. "We'll make do until the furniture comes."

"Hmm."

She took another breath. "Right now, all I want is to stand in the garden of our new home and admire the view! Come on. Let me show you everything."

Butterflies fluttered in her belly and tickled her throat as she opened the car and got out.

Even though they had to sell their apartment in San Jose to afford the cottage, the house had been cheap compared to other places. The reason for the relatively low price was the seller's condition that they'd buy the small house sight unseen and in as-is condition. The agent had reassured them that it was only because the owner didn't want to be disturbed and that the house was in fine condition.

Hannah could no longer wait for her husband; she had to stand in the garden right now, just as she had in her childhood. She ran ahead, right into the midst of the colorful riot of blossoms and flowers and petals and leaves.

Evan's door slammed shut, and his footsteps came after her. "Hannah. Wait."

The sun was hot on her naked arms and neck as she turned, and she felt radiant with joy and excitement. "Darling, really, I don't mind. We'll sleep on the floor tonight, like two young lovebirds who just bought their first house!"

Hannah beamed at him. That's exactly what she wanted—a new beginning. A second chance at love and happiness and *togetherness*. She couldn't remember the last time they'd slept with each other. Two months ago? Maybe three? Evan's job had gobbled up his time and energy in the last year, and she'd not wanted to add to it with demands for intimacy. Of course, the many years of unsuccessfully trying to conceive a baby had not added joy in the bedroom. It hadn't been long before sleeping together had become a chore, an item on the to-do list, an embarrassing necessity rather than an act of love.

But tonight would be the night when Hannah would be brave. She'd rekindle her husband's desire once and for all.

She held out a hand, blinking into the bright sun. "Shall we go inside and explore our new home?" According to the agent, not much had changed since Hannah's mother had to sell the house. And Hannah couldn't wait to show her husband everything, to remember her happy, sunny childhood in this house that she still loved so much.

Standing between the golden poppies that swayed in the warm sea breeze, Evan ran a hand through his hair. "Hannah."

Hannah shaded her eyes to see him better. He was being weird. "What, Evan?"

He pushed his hands into his pockets. "We're not going inside."

Confused, she dropped her hand. "We're not? Did you forget to pick up the key from the agent?"

"No." A breath blew up his ribs, and then he exhaled in a rush. "I'm sorry, Hannah."

"Sorry about what?" The joyful butterflies in her stomach dropped like little cold raindrops, one by one. She put a hand to her belly, hating the feeling of anxiety sneaking into her happy new start. "What's going on?"

Evan moistened his lips. "I can't do this, Hannah. I can't... I just can't do it anymore."

"Do what anymore?" The butterflies didn't turn into raindrops but ice. Her insides froze as the frost glazing her stomach crawled toward her heart, her throat, her voice.

"Be with you. I'm done. I'm—Hannah, I'm done. I'm sorry."

"You're done?" Her words were whispers, whisked away by the breeze before they reached her husband.

"I've been done for a long time." He spread his hands to underline his words. "I tried. Believe me, I tried. I wanted this to be the new...but it's not. And I can't pretend any longer." He dropped his hands in a final gesture of giving up. "I want a divorce, Hannah."

Divorce.

The word echoed around the garden and the sky, bouncing from the tufts of lavender to the cotton puff clouds in the bright blue sky and back.

Hannah grabbed at an old rhododendron bough to steady herself in a reeling world. "You want a divorce." She didn't need to ask. She knew her husband well enough to know he was serious.

"I'm sorry. I guess this comes as a shock. I should've... I thought I could make it work. But I have to stop living a lie."

"A lie?" Something like anger curdled in her icy stomach. "Our life is a *lie* to you?" She knew he meant what he was saying. And yet, Hannah couldn't believe her ears.

"I should have told you before. I understand that, Hannah. I really hoped I could fix this. But I cannot. It's over."

Hannah didn't know where to start. After staring at him for too long, she held out her hand. The ice inside her was melting, giving rise to a wave of nausea. "Give me the key, Evan. You can go back to San Jose. We'll talk tomorrow."

Evan took another deep breath. "Well...the house is in my name, Hannah. *I* bought it with money *I* earned from working hard at my job. So...I'm the one who is staying. *You* can go back to San Jose. Take the car and the contents of the missing moving truck."

"I can...what? I can take the car and the furniture?"

He nodded, avoiding her eyes. "It's mostly your books and a few filing cabinets, actually," he said. "The other furniture is already in the house."

"Why? Why, Evan?"

At first, she thought he wasn't going to answer. But then he cleared his throat. "You read your little stories to seniors and kids, Hannah," he said, his voice quiet but firm. "For ten years, you've mucked around with board books while I worked my pants off to pay the bills. It's only fair that I get the house."

Hannah blinked. "I *mucked* around with board books? I'm a librarian, Evan. Even if I didn't earn as much as you, I worked too." A year ago, her position had been downsized when funding was cut. But she'd still worked the same hours, volunteering her time to the library and the community.

"Go back to San Jose and stay with your friend Amanda until the divorce is sorted." Defiant, Evan raised his head to meet her eyes.

Amanda had moved to Oregon six months ago. But it didn't matter. "And then?" Hannah whispered. Not because she wanted to know, but because she wanted to see how far he was prepared to take this.

He shrugged. "And then we each do whatever it is we'll do with our life," he said. "I'm sorry to break this to you on your birthday, Hannah. I wish I'd made up my mind earlier. But it's been coming for a long while. Years, really." He crossed his arms. "This,"—he looked around the beautiful garden, the gorgeous sea, the charming house—"is my new start."

Hannah pressed her lips together to keep them from trembling. She couldn't cry now. "It's *my* childhood home, Evan," she whispered. "I love this place." *I love you*, were the words she swallowed, together with a sob rising as burning hot and insuppressible as lava from her churning chest.

The stony look in his eyes made her let go of the rhododendron and take a step back. "Sorry, Hannah," he said harshly. "Wanting something and getting it are two different things. You're no longer that cutie who can point at stuff with big blue eyes and get it. I'm done with that. I'm *done*."

Hannah's eyes widened at the cruel words. When had she ever done that? Not once. Not once had she pointed at something and expected to simply get it. Not after being raised by a single mom who desperately struggled to keep their home and was forced to sell anyway just to feed her daughter.

"I thought we were a team, Evan." Her voice was that of a stranger. Calm and toneless, the words like dry pebbles hitting the asphalt of an empty road. "I thought we were in this together. We can work through this."

"I know you do. But it takes two people to play this game, and it's too late." Evan's eyes lost their glare as he tossed her the car keys. She didn't catch them, and they fell into a clump of beach daisies by her feet.

He cleared his throat. "It's better if you don't come in before you leave," he said. "I'm sorry. But it's about time you stop dreaming and face reality, Hannah. You're middle-aged, unemployed, barren. I have to finally move forward with my life."

CHAPTER 2

Someone knocked on the window, startling Hannah. She lifted her head off the steering wheel and rolled down the window. "Yeah?"

"Hi." A young woman wearing a black half-apron smiled at her. "Hi. I don't want to...but are you okay?"

"Yeah." Hannah nodded because she couldn't smile. Her eyes were so dry they hurt. She blinked. "I'm sorry. Did I park in the wrong spot?"

"No, you're fine. Um—I work in the restaurant here." The young woman thrust a thumb over her shoulder at the building behind her. "I've seen you sit here for over an hour, and I thought I'd ask if you'd like a coffee and some cake? It's fresh out of the oven."

"Oh." Hannah rubbed her dry eyes and took a shallow breath. She couldn't take deep ones anymore; she'd discovered that when she'd pulled over. Evan had quite literally taken her breath away. "Thank you. But I don't think so." The nausea had stuck around, even if her husband hadn't.

The young woman nodded thoughtfully. "Are you from Mendocino Cove? I don't recognize you. Are you visiting?"

Hannah's fingers gripped the steering wheel tighter, blanching the knuckles. "I grew up just over the hill in Mendocino Beach, actually." *I have a house there. I finally bought my mother's house back.* She gritted her teeth.

"Well, it's just that my boss baked a cream torte this morning," the woman said after a short pause. "I came up with the recipe, and we haven't sold any yet. Would you do me a huge favor and try it? I need someone unbiased to have a piece and tell us if it's any good."

"You do?" A small smile tugged on Hannah's lips, even though it didn't make its way to her heart. If it was a lie, at least it was a charming lie.

"Do you mind? It's on the house, of course. By the way, my name's Zoe."

"I'm Hannah." Without her doing, the smile widened on her lips. What else did she have to do? She didn't even know where to go next. She had half a tank of gas, a credit card that she prayed would still work, and a truckload of books stuck on a mountain somewhere. "All right."

"Great!" Zoe stepped back to make space on the narrow sidewalk.

Hannah got out of the car and followed the young woman into the restaurant. There was a sun-flooded second level with great views of the ocean, and she was shown to a table by the window.

Feeling cold and shivery even though it was a warm day, Hannah put her purse on the back of her chair and sat quietly to look around. There were other people up here, women mostly, groups of friends that were laughing and chatting and eating cakes that must be other cakes than the experiment Hannah was supposed to try.

Despite the cheery, happy atmosphere, Hannah felt out of place. Whenever one of the guests caught her eye, they smiled and nodded. Hannah did her best to smile and nod back, but it felt strange and detached. Nevertheless, after a while of this, Hannah relaxed enough to drop her tight shoulders and turn to hold her face into the sun.

"Here you go." Zoe was back, setting a large glass of creamy coffee and a plate with the most enormous slice of cream torte on the table. "It's my raspberry white chocolate mousse torte and a mocha affogato from our new machine. I hope you don't mind trying it—you really are our guinea pig."

Hannah stared at the torte. She'd only had a gas-station blueberry muffin when they left San Jose at dawn, and now it was going on noon. But even though she was hungry, she didn't feel like eating. Let alone that much. And also... "Um." She looked up, uncertain whether there'd been a misunderstanding. "I'm not sure my credit card works. We should probably check it first."

The young woman's eyes softened. "I meant it when I said it's on the house! Believe me, you're doing me a favor by trying it." She winked and left, hurrying back to the kitchen.

"That's nice of you," Hannah murmured, too late. For a moment, her eyes prickled as some little moisture returned, and she blinked.

She couldn't stop eating because Evan was throwing a tantrum. He'd been thoughtless before. And while he'd never acted this cruelly, or talked about divorce, or told her to go away, she'd developed some ground rules on how to deal with his moods.

Rule number one was to carry on carrying on.

Hannah picked up her fork and slowly plunged it into the luscious cake. Layers of white chocolate sponge cake were filled with airy, ruby-red mousse and frosted with a dark ganache. Soft and fluffy and creamy, it smelled of the cool, crunchy chocolate and sweet, warm raspberries.

Despite her misery, she couldn't help but be curious about the taste.

Hannah scooped up a bite. When she tasted it, it was like stepping into an orchestra playing in full swing. A symphony of sun-soaked sweetness and creamy-rich indulgence, fruity freshness and chocolaty luxury danced over her tongue.

"Hmm!" Surprised, she covered her mouth with her fingertips as the bite melted away like a sweet summer day. How was she even capable of sensations like these in a moment like this? She took another bite, savoring it, and then she set down her fork to try the coffee.

It wasn't just coffee, she quickly found out. It was a tall glass filled with velvety smooth espresso, infused with rich white chocolate syrup and a hint of raspberry liqueur. The steaming hot espresso was poured over a generous scoop of creamy vanilla bean ice cream, causing it to melt and mingle with the coffee in a luscious swirl of flavors. Topped with a dollop of freshly whipped cream, a drizzle of raspberry coulis, and a sprinkle of white chocolate shavings, the decadent coffee was the perfect match for the cream torte.

Hannah sipped and ate her way through her sweet meal, and for a few minutes, Evan, her mother's house, and even the divorce hid behind a curtain of berries and cream and the kindness of strangers.

"How was it?" Zoe had returned.

"It was—" Hannah opened her mouth, but she was full of cream and short of words. "It was so, so good," she concluded finally. "I needed this. Your recipe is excellent, Zoe."

"Good! I'm glad." Smiling, the young woman picked up the empty plate and glass. "Where are you staying tonight?"

"In San Jose. Um. Actually... I don't know." Embarrassment warmed Hannah's cheeks. She didn't want to drive back. Once the mountain range separated her from Evan, and the house, and Mendocino Beach, it was all over. That's what it felt like, anyway.

"Do you need a hotel? There's a nice one here in Mendocino Cove. It's pretty booked this summer, but I'm friends with the owners. I'm sure they'll find you a room."

"That's...again, with the credit card." Hannah fell back in her chair, feeling her face crumple. "We were going to move into my mother's old house today. My husband just told me he wants a divorce. He took the house, and I..." A shiver ran through her, shaking her shoulders, as her denial melted away. "He gave me the car. And some furniture, but it's in a truck stuck on the mountain somewhere."

The other woman's eyes widened. "He can't do that!"

Hannah swallowed. "He did."

Zoe pressed her lips together so hard they formed a white line. "What are you going to do, honey?"

Hannah wasn't used to young women calling her honey. But it was nice. Between the whipped cream, the raspberry mousse, and the honey, a tight screw trapping her rib cage loosened. She sighed, glad to be able to draw more air. "I don't know," she admitted. "I have no idea. I can't tell if he's really being serious."

"Do you still have family in the area?"

"My mother moved to San Jose a long time ago," Hannah said. "I have no other relatives." She scratched her nose. "I think I'll call my mom." She looked up. "Yeah. I'll call my mom." She smiled, and this time, it didn't feel mechanical.

"I'll get you another coffee," Zoe said. "Something nice."

"I'd love to, but I'm stuffed. I simply can't drink more."

Zoe smiled back. "You can try." She left and returned as promised with another glass a few moments later. "I'm having way too much fun with these," she murmured to herself as she set it in front of Hannah. With a nod, she went to the neighboring table, where the ladies had finished their own coffees and cakes and were clamoring for attention.

Despite being full, Hannah took a sip. Below a thick layer of steamed milk foam dusted with cocoa powder and garnished with a sprinkle of toasted hazelnut crumbs was smooth hot coffee. This time, it was infused with the rich, nutty, comforting sweetness of amaretto liqueur and a hint of hazelnut syrup. Dabbing the foam and cocoa off her lips with a napkin, Hannah pulled out her phone to call her mother.

When she looked at the screen, she spotted a text from Evan waiting for her.

Hannah's heart jumped like a startled deer. With shaking fingers, she tapped on the notification.

CHAPTER 3

H*ope you're okay*, Evan's text read. And then her husband of ten years gave Hannah the telephone number for their moving company so she could call the truck full of her books that was stuck on the mountain.

Hannah's breath had just returned, but now it vanished again as if she'd been punched, leaving her gasping for air. She had expected an apology. A note asking her to come back to the house, they should talk. At least that. *At least* an invitation to talk.

With a trembling finger, she dialed her mother's number.

"Sweetheart!" Her mother's voice was jubilantly happy. "Happy birthday! I was going to call you earlier, but I thought you'd be busy with the move! How are you?"

Hannah's lips formed the word *divorce*, but she couldn't utter them. Not yet. "How are *you?*" she instead asked back. "How is the cruise?"

"It's fantastic! The sea, the ocean? It's *super*. So is the food! But how is Mendocino Beach? Still the same? Are you there yet? How is our little house? I can't believe the dates for your move and my cruise crossed like that!

The minute I'm back, I'll come to visit!" She laughed. "That still gives you a whole month to settle, darling!"

"The house is beautiful," Hannah spoke softly. No need to burden the happy ladies one table over with her tale. "But—I can't go in, Mom. There's been a problem."

"What problem? Did they not air the attic? I told them when I sold it that they needed to air it out! Is it mold? Is it black mold? Tell me that's not it!"

"Mom, it's okay. I'm taking care of it. I don't want you to worry." Hannah still simply couldn't say the word divorce out loud. Or tell her mother that she'd lost them their beloved cottage once again. "But right now, I don't have a place to stay."

"Well, where's your hubby?"

"He's got to go to San Francisco for work," Hannah said hastily. It wasn't much of a lie since Evan frequently did just that. "I only need a place for a few days so I can find something else. A week, maybe."

The wind crackling in the line suddenly stopped. "Honey, of course I'd say take my apartment in San Jose," her mother said. "But I rented out."

"You did?" Hannah pressed her lips together. She didn't want to go back to San Jose, but still. In the back of her mind, her mother's empty apartment had been a lifeline. A place to lick her wounds until she figured out what to do next.

"I know, I know. I didn't tell you because I *knew* you'd say it was too risky, having strangers in there and all that..."

"I wouldn't have said that," Hannah said, aware that she sounded prickly.

"Well, maybe not, but either way, honey. I put it on one of those websites and bam, a couple rented it. They need a base to do some house hunting in the area. She's *really* pregnant, and it's a lot of money for me, sweetheart. I thought I'd go ahead."

Hannah pulled herself together. Her mother had never had any money. The cruise had been a present from her girlfriends for her seventieth birthday. If she could make the apartment pay for itself while she was gone, it was a no-brainer. "Well, of course. It's fine." Hannah tried to sound cheerful.

"I should have told you, sweetheart. Uh, there's no hotel in Mendocino Beach as far as I know, but there used to be a big old place in the cove, run by a real character. I'm sure she's not there anymore, but maybe try that? Or—you know, the owner of the bookstore in town used to rent out the apartment on top of his store! Of course that's also twenty years ago now." She laughed. "But maybe it's still there. You could check it out. You do like books."

"I do. It's all right, Mom. I'll have a look around. I'll figure it out." They exchanged a few more words about Hannah's birthday, her mother's cabin, the captain, the dress code, and the dinner buffets, and then they ended the call because Mom gleefully announced that she had to go get a pedicure.

Zoe returned to pick up the empty coffee glass. "Are you ready for lunch, by any chance? My boss makes a fine lobster roll."

"I'm sure he does, but I couldn't try to eat one more thing. No matter how delicious." Hannah picked up her purse and rose. "I'll come back to pay for all this once I sort things out. I know you didn't need me to try out a new cake. It was much too good to be an experiment."

"Nope, no worries, Hannah," Zoe said comfortably. "Every cake is an experiment. And nobody sits crying in front of the Mermaid Galley on my watch. Even if there are no tears."

Impulsively, Hannah opened her arms and pulled the young woman into a hug. She wasn't feeling good, but she was feeling a whole lot better than before. "Thank you," she murmured. "You are marvelous. You have no idea how much I needed you to come along."

Zoe hugged her back, and then she pulled a napkin with a phone number from her apron pocket. "This is the number of the hotel I told you about. If you call, tell them I sent you. They'll make space for you even if they're booked. Even if, heaven forbid, your credit card glitches out on you."

"Thank you very much." Grateful, Hannah took the napkin and slipped it into her pocket.

"What are you going to do now?"

"I'm going back to Mendocino Beach," Hannah declared, surprising herself with this resolution. But there was no way she was going to leave her hometown so easily. "I want to talk to my husband before I leave."

"Good idea. Come here anytime you need a pick-me-up. Take care of yourself, Hannah." Zoe nodded, smiled, and then she went to the next table.

Hannah took a short walk over the bluff that led to the ocean. It was wild and swept down to the ocean much like the one by her mother's old cottage. Only here, the ground was covered with wildflowers instead of a garden. Bright orange poppies dotted the dry grass like soft little suns, towering spikes of purple and blue lupines swayed in the breeze, and delicate clusters of pink sea thrift peppered the dry grass, their tufted blooms looking like tiny cotton candy clouds.

Steep, sandy paths with frayed grassy edges led down to the cove's half-moon beach, and for a long while, Hannah stood and looked down the bluff. A young family was on the beach, the kids playing with their dad in the shallow water. The mother was reading on a beach towel, her sun hat shading her face. She turned the pages quickly, spellbound by the story.

Suddenly, Hannah knew what to do.

She turned on her heel and walked back up the bluff, to her car that was still parked in front of the restaurant.

She'd find out whether the vacation apartment over the bookstore still existed. As a child, the bookstore had been Hannah's favorite place. However poor they were, her mother somehow always found the money to buy Hannah a book.

Maybe it was the reason why the old store with its rows of tall bookshelves and cozy, overstuffed chairs, the creaking wood floor and crackling fireplace had been the one place where Hannah felt rich and wealthy. In the soft light filtering through the dusty windows, everything was possible. She and Mom used to walk over once a week on a Saturday and cuddle up in one of the chairs, sampling books until they decided on one that suited them both. They'd proudly buy it, and Hannah was allowed to carry it home and keep it on the shelf over her bed.

In the evening, after they'd eaten and cleared away the dishes, they went into the garden. Hannah played hopscotch or searched for pink shells on the beach. Mom weeded the flower beds or picket berries, waving whenever Hannah looked up at the house. When the sun finally sank into the ocean, Hannah climbed back up the bluff, and they'd sit down on the old wooden bench under the rhododendron to watch the sky turn into molten gold and fire.

Once the last sliver of the sun had sunk into the wild waters, the blue hour settled over the coast. "Storytime," Mom would say and smile at Hannah, and Hannah would jump up and run to get the new book. They took turns reading chapters. Mom with the voice and fluency of the trained actor that she was, and Hannah with the hesitant, halting pace and inflection of a new reader.

Remembering story time on the old bench, Hannah slipped into the sun-warmed car that still smelled of Evan's licorice. She rolled down the window and started the engine.

She and her mother had been poor, but all Hannah's life she'd yearned to reclaim the harmony and peace of their life in that cottage by the sea. And now, just when it was about to happen, Evan wanted to give up on her. On *them*.

Hannah pulled out of the cove and back onto the street to Mendocino Beach when the dam burst. The tears that had been so conspicuously absent until now streamed in a torrent down her cheeks and her nose, dripping off the tip and landing in fat, dark splotches on her jeans. Twice she had to pull over because she couldn't see, and sobs racked her to the point where it wasn't safe to drive. But each time, she waited until the surge was over, and then she carried on.

That was another thing she'd learned from her mother. Carry on. Whatever it is, it's never desperate. Not when Dad died. Not when they lost the house. And not now.

By the time Hannah pulled into Mendocino Beach's Main Street, the tears had trickled to a stop and only started back up when she thought of Evan's words and the stony look in his eyes when he told her that he had already moved on.

Sniffling, she took a corner. She'd only been back in Mendocino Beach one or two times since her childhood. It was a long trip, and staying the night in the nearby towns of Maytown or Pebble Beach quickly got expensive. Because of the money, it had always come down to a choice between visiting either Hannah's childhood town or another place they both wanted to go to.

Evan's vote typically tipped the scales in favor of the latter.

But Hannah instinctively knew her way around the sunbaked streets and lanes. And while everything seemed to be a little bit smaller, or wider, or farther, or closer than she remembered, it didn't take her long to find the old bookstore.

Hannah parked the car and brushed her sleeve across her face, erasing the last traces of tears. With a deep breath, she stepped out, purposefully planting her feet on the sandy ground of Mendocino Beach.

CHAPTER 4

"Hello? Is there anyone here?" Hannah gently pulled the door of the bookstore closed behind her. The sight of the old shelves, still filled with rows of blue, red, and golden spines that guarded tales of magic, love, and courage, instantly soothed her.

"Hi." A man sat behind the counter. Not the old man who used to sell books to her nine-year-old self. This one was younger, in the prime of male middle age. Now he stood, setting the book he'd been reading on the counter.

Distracted as Hannah was, she couldn't help but notice the man's striking presence. Standing tall at six feet with a lean, muscular build, he commanded attention. His broad shoulders and strong, chiseled features might have intimidated her under different circumstances, but the eye patch covering one of his piercing blue eyes softened his appearance.

"Can I help you?" he asked. "Looking for anything in particular? Romances are in the middle. Clean on the left, smutty to the right." He nodded significantly. "I don't judge either way."

"That's a relief." A smile relaxed the muscles of Hannah's face, still taut from her crying spell. "But I didn't come for a book. I suppose..." She took a breath. What was she going to say exactly? Maybe she could ask if he could check if the credit card still worked?

"You suppose what?" The new bookkeeper shifted his weight to the other foot. His stance was wary, as if he was ready to either run or attack.

Hannah tried again. "I used to live in town as a child," she said. "Obviously, it's been a hot second." It came out sounding like an apology.

Maybe she was wrong. But it was possible that the corner of his lips twitched. "Same," he said.

"Oh." She had no memory of his face. "Um. I'm afraid I'm in a bit of a predicament. I had planned to move to Mendocino Beach today." Her voice gave out. She tore her gaze from the blue eye that wasn't covered by the eye patch and cleared her throat. "But it's not working out after all. So now I don't have a place to stay."

The blue eye narrowed cautiously. "Do you need a self-help book?"

Her smile returned. This time, it felt a bit more natural. "I probably need that and also a romance," she admitted. "But what I meant to ask—there used to be a room for rent on top of the store. That's not still there, is it?" Hopeful, she looked up.

He was chewing on the inside corner of his mouth. "What if it is?"

"Then...I have a credit card." Her heart sank as she fumbled for the wallet in her purse. There wasn't much in their account after purchasing the house. But a little bit. Enough to live for a month or two.

Unless Evan had decided to take that too.

Hannah closed the distance between her and the bookseller and held out the card.

"Thank you." The man took it, holding the small plastic rectangle awkwardly in his fingers before he gingerly sat it on the counter between them. "What do you want me to do with this?"

Despite everything, Hannah felt her smile deepen even more; the man sounded so worried. "I'm sorry," she said and tapped on the card. "Sorry. Let me start again. My name is Hannah..." She swallowed her married name. It tasted bitter in the back of her throat and burned going down. "Banner." Her maiden name would do for now.

"Hannah Ban—" His features suddenly relaxed, and he grinned boyishly.

It took her a moment. "Oh. Right. Hannah Banana. Yep—that's me." She grinned back. The mild sting of the old nickname was long gone. "I guess we did both grow up in town, even if I don't remember you."

"I'm Alex. Alex Everett."

Hannah moistened her lips nervously, trying to remember.

"No?"

She shook her head. "I'm sorry."

"Oh well. Can't win 'em all." The bookseller leaned over and propped his elbows on the counter. "I do remember the curls. What's up, Hannah? What brings you back to town? Like you said, it's been a while."

"So, I...we...my husband and I bought back my mother's old house on Sunset Lane," she said haltingly. "But um...well, not that I want to air my dirty laundry or anything, but he told me a couple of hours ago that he wants a divorce. And he's taking the house, and I...I don't have anywhere to stay right now. So I thought... I don't want to leave just yet." She hesitated, crossing her fingers for good luck. "I thought maybe I could rent the room above the store for a night or two? If it's empty. If it still exists."

"It still exists." Alex looked down at his folded hands.

"It does?" Again she had to smile. That was three smiles in three minutes. After the crying spell, it felt good.

"I just returned home myself." He pointed a thumb at his eye patch. "Got injured in action."

"Oh no." Shocked, Hannah covered her mouth. Losing her eyesight was one of the big fears in her life. She couldn't imagine not being able to read everything all the time. "I'm so sorry. Military?" Everything about him said military; the buzz cut that was starting to grow out, the wary stance, the muscular frame that was too toned for everyday life.

He nodded. "Afghanistan."

"Thank you for your service." She meant it, but the words didn't seem enough. "I'm really sorry your eye was injured."

For the first time, he smiled. But when he spoke, his words were clipped. "I got off easy." He straightened back up. "So, I haven't been up in the apartment much. It's a bit messy." He pushed the credit card back across the counter. "Tell you what. You can stay up there if you clean it up. I might rent it out later. Not now. I have to deal with other things first."

Half a boulder rolled off Hannah's heart. "Thank you," she said. "That's very generous of you. I'll be happy to clean the place." She tried to pick up the credit card. But the flat plastic seemed glued to the counter, and her short nails slipped off the edges several times.

"Hmm." He picked it up without effort and handed it to her.

"Thanks," she mumbled and let her shoulder-length hair cover her face. "I'm not always this clumsy."

"You used to be," he said, but when she looked up, surprised he remembered anything like that, he cleared his throat. "Right. Stay right here. I need ten. Didn't know you were going to show up when you did."

"Sure. Go ahead." She turned to inspect the bookstore while he was gone. She remembered the armchairs. They were still the same ones, their pattern no more or less worn than when she'd been nine years old.

Alex came back inside. "Come on," he said, his voice gruff. "Let's have a look upstairs. But don't expect much. I'm not running a B&B. I can barely take care of myself."

"I don't expect anything," she promised and followed him into a break room behind the counter. There were wooden kitchen chairs, a sink with a few mugs, an ancient fridge, a bowl with a bunch of bananas, and a huge jar of peanut butter on a kitchen table. The only new thing besides the food was an expensive Italian coffee machine that claimed most of the narrow counter space.

Alex picked a pair of keys from an old-fashioned keyboard next to the door and scratched the stubble on his chin. "I think that's the one." Without waiting for a response, he turned and took another door, and another, until suddenly they were outside in the alley behind the bookstore.

"Point in favor: it has its own entrance." Alex stopped at the bottom of a flight of stairs leading to a weathered door. The green paint of the door was cracked from sun and salt and wind, but the warm, worn wood looked solid and reassuring. Behind this door, Hannah felt, was the safe haven she desperately needed right now.

"Like I said, I don't come up here. Got something wrong with my knee on top of the eye." Alex held out the key.

"I'm so sorry."

"It is what it is."

"Sure." She picked the key from his open palm. It was old and bearded, the metal warm and heavy and just as reassuring as the door to which it belonged. "I'll make sure to clean it up."

Again, the almost-smile tugged on the corner of his mouth. "I'd be obliged. I kind of thought I heard the pitter-patter of little feet over my head today, so don't get scared if a coon jumps out at you."

She tilted her head. "Are you joking? I can't tell."

He sighed. "I can't tell either. Good luck. And remember that you don't have to take it if you don't want it. Just drop off the key in the store, and we're good." Without waiting for a reply, he turned and left.

Hannah looked after him, only now noticing the limp dragging on his step. She bit her lip. He probably had difficulty getting up the stairs to the apartment.

When Alex disappeared around the corner, Hannah climbed the stairs and unlocked the green door. With a feeling of relief, she stepped inside. Diffuse light filtered through gauzy curtains drawn before the windows, dousing the small studio in a warm, amber light that played on the old wooden planks of the wood floor. She took a step, listening to the comfortable creak as the boards registered her weight. It was warm, and when she closed her eyes and took a breath, the air smelled of old books and faded pages, worn vellum covers and tea leaves.

A sound startled her eyes open again. Hannah exhaled and held her breath to listen. The rushing of the ocean came from the open door, but there was also something else. She tilted her head, and when she finally figured out the source of the sound, she smiled with relief.

It wasn't a raccoon.

It was Alex, walking into the bookstore below.

CHAPTER 5

Holding the book open on the page picturing antique patterns of ocean waves, Sara turned to see who had entered the bookstore from the back.

"Hey, Alex! Good to see you." She smiled when she saw that the bookstore's owner had returned. The ex-marine had only recently opened the old bookstore again, but she liked him already. Despite his gruff demeanor and unshaven chin, despite the jeans and T-shirt look that never changed, despite the grumpy silences that often met her curious questions.

"Hi, Sara." Alex nodded once before he settled onto the chair behind the counter and picked up his own book. A military novel, Sara knew, that had kept him busy for a week now. She'd wondered why reading took him so long until one day she asked, and he shared that his good eye couldn't keep going the way it used to. He had to rest and relax it to make sure it didn't tire to the point where it gave him headaches. When she'd asked why he wasn't listening to audiobooks, he'd only said that he needed to hold that paper in his hands.

Same.

She held up the book on graphic design she'd spotted in the used-books section of the store. It had been tucked in between a Manga comic and the speeches of Marcus Aurelius. "You didn't tell me you had this."

He raised an eyebrow without looking up. "I didn't know you wanted it."

"It's a classic. Of course I want it." She came to the counter and set the book down, tapping her finger on it. "How much are we talking?"

"For you? Thirty bucks." He looked up and grinned, letting her know he was teasing.

"Fifteen. Thank you very much." She smiled and pulled out her wallet. Fifteen was a good price. The book was used, earmarked, and there were notes scribbled on the pages.

"Fine." He held out a hand, and she put the bills in it. "I could get more books along the lines of this one if you're looking for graphic design and patterns. The graduates from Lizzie May university are getting rid of their textbooks."

It wasn't like Sara had no money. She had a good job as a paralegal assistant. But she was the only breadwinner in a family of four. If she could get used books instead of paying the sticker price of new ones, she couldn't afford to pass up the opportunity. "Yes, please. Let me know if something like this comes along." Sara slipped the thick book into her farmers market bag.

Alex crossed his arms and leaned back, tipping his stool on the back legs. "Do you draw?"

"Uh." Sara hitched the strap higher and sighed. "I wish I could. I used to, before the kids. Back in the day, you know?"

He nodded. "No more time for hobbies?"

"No more time," she confirmed. "I'm lucky that my boss lets me work as many hours as I want."

"The elusive Julian Sterling."

"He's not elusive. You just haven't been in town that long."

"So then what? Is he being cheap on you?"

"No, not at all. But I have two expensive teenagers and my husband was laid off in the pandemic. My parents and in-laws drop in whenever they want to, and frankly, our mortgage is higher than it should be. We weren't able to refinance when we should have done."

"Shoot." He shook his head.

"Yeah, I know." Feeling a twinge of guilt for indulging herself and spending money unnecessarily, Sara patted the bag that held her used treasure. "I really shouldn't drool over pretty wallpaper patterns."

Alex shrugged. His blue eye—the one not covered by his patch—watched her intently. "There's money in graphic design. Isn't there?"

"If you can do websites and advertisements and are able to hustle up clients. But I already have a job. My problem is that I'm an artist at heart. Not an accomplished one, that's not what I'm saying. But somewhere buried deep under thick layers of calendars and manila folders and case files burns the soul of a wild child."

She grinned and knocked on the counter. "Know what I mean?"

"No." Alex let his chair fall back forward and lifted his military novel. "I don't know a thing about wild children or the shady corners of your soul. Sorry."

Unbothered, Sara tugged the elastic waistband of her floral skirt back in place. "Just because your fiancé ditched you doesn't mean all of us are horrible, Alex. My soul is not shadowy. There are no corners. It's a sunny, airy, wide-open place."

He lowered his book. "A sunny, airy, wide-open space that's buried by calendars and...what was it? Manila folders?"

"Yes," she confirmed. "That's exactly right. Manila folders."

The front door creaked open, and she turned around. A woman her own age—middle age, which would be the best age of them all if Sara didn't feel so tired and broke—entered the store. Her sky-blue eyes were cautious, and her brown curls, with a striking silver accent framing her face, were tousled by the sea breeze.

"Sorry," the woman said nervously, looking from Sara to Alex. "Is this a good time?"

"Yes, it is. Hi," Sara said eagerly. She loved meeting new women with girlfriend potential. "Who are you?"

Alex rose. "Come in, Hannah."

"Hannah...Hannah Banana?" Sara felt her eyes widen. Now that she had a name, she remembered the face. "Uh, don't tell me...Sunset Lane!"

Hannah nodded and joined her and Alex at the counter. "That's right. I'm so sorry, I don't have a memory for faces."

"Sara Reynolds. You might remember me as Silly Sara."

Hannah's face broke into a smile. "Silly Sara! I remember now! Of course." She held out a hand. "How are you, Sara?"

Sara shook the hand. Hannah's fingers clasped her with a firm grip, but not so firm it felt like she was trying to make a point. Sara liked a handshake like that, especially in a potential girlfriend. She smiled back. "I'm good! Married, two kids who are almost grown, parents alive and growing more peculiar by the day. And you?"

A shadow settled on the pretty blue eyes and lowered the nose that hadn't lengthened much since fourth grade. "My husband told me this morning that he wants a divorce." She blinked and quickly covered her mouth, as if she hadn't meant to let the words slip out.

"For real?" Sara put her farmers market bag with the heavy textbook back on the counter. She had to be back at Sterling Law in ten minutes and hadn't had lunch yet. But clearly, this was an emergency. "He literally just told you?"

Hannah dropped her hand and nodded. "It's okay," she murmured. "I'm okay."

"It's okay? You're okay with it?" Sara knew she should leave and get back to filing whatever it was she needed to file. But over the years, she'd often wondered what had become of Hannah Banana. And a fresh divorce announcement was more interesting than a dispute over property lines any day.

"Sara," Alex grumbled. "Don't you have to get back?"

"I do, but come *on*." Sara shook her head at him. "Your husband told you literally just now?"

"Um. Well, two hours ago. The thing is..." Hannah looked uncertain, like she didn't know about Sara.

Sara was used to the look. She got it all the time, for asking questions, for being invested, for caring. Of course she was nosy. Why shouldn't she be? She always meant well.

"What's the thing?" she probed when Hannah didn't continue.

"We just bought back my mother's house," Hannah said in a small voice. "And Evan said...he said it was his. His name is on the deed, and he paid for it. He gave me the car."

A tidal wave of sisterly outrage swept over Sara. "He gave you the car? How long have you been married?"

"Ten years," Hannah said and cleared her throat a couple of times.

"How is the apartment?" Alex asked loudly, throwing a grim look at Sara.

"He can't just do that," Sara said, ignoring him. "He can't just tell you what's his and what's yours. This is California. You need to talk to a lawyer."

"I don't want a divorce," Hannah said quickly. "And I had no idea that he did. I thought we were pretty happy and at the start of a beautiful new life."

"Oh," Sara said. Her heart filled with pity. Divorce cases where one partner was taken by surprise always got to her. Well, to be honest, they got to her when it was the woman who was taken by surprise. Men rarely saw it coming, but usually, their wives had told them several times a day for the last twenty years.

Hannah pushed her hair out of her face, revealing a dust smudge on her cheek. "Um, Alex, the apartment is lovely. If there are raccoons, I haven't found them yet. You don't happen to have a broom I could borrow, do you?"

Sara's eyes widened. So Hannah was staying upstairs?

"I do have a broom. I even know where it is. One moment." He went into the back to get it. "Anything else?" he asked when he came back with it.

Hannah took the broom. "I'd like to buy a book," she said timidly. Or maybe not timid, Sara thought. Maybe timid was the wrong word. Beaten down. "Reading is my escape, but all my books are stuck in a truck on the mountain. The truck has engine damage, and it'll be a while before it will get down to the coast."

"What about your phone?" Sara asked. "Don't you read on your phone?"

Alex groaned, and Hannah blinked. "I don't have a charger," she said. "I'll have to order one, and I don't want to use my phone too much until then. I'll need it for making calls."

Both Sara and Alex offered their chargers, but it turned out that they used different brands that were not compatible with Hannah's old phone.

"Right. What do you like to read?" Alex asked when the charger question was settled.

"Anything, really." Hannah glanced at the shelves. "Though maybe not a romance right now."

"Maybe a mystery?" Sara suggested. "I'm reading one right now. Lots of great characters, not too much gore, and a detective who may or may not survive her personal life."

Hannah smiled. "That sounds good, actually."

Alex pointed at a shelf, and Sara went to get Hannah a copy of the book she was reading.

"Thank you." Hannah pulled out her credit card. "Can you please charge it?"

"It's all right. The book has a dog's ear."

"It clearly doesn't," Hannah said softly. "It's a pristine copy."

"Hey, it's on me, Hannah," Sara said quickly. Alex was already losing money on the store; one boring day in the office, Sara had estimated his profit to see if he needed help. He did, and Sara was trying to think on how to do it.

But she'd just remembered something about Hannah. "Hey, Hannah! Did you know our grandmothers had a book club? Your grandma and mine were in it, and also a couple of other ladies."

"I didn't know that!" Hannah's brows lifted in surprise.

Sara nodded. "I have my grandma's journal somewhere at home; I can show you. It's the cutest thing."

"I'd love to see it," Hannah said, brightening. "I barely knew my grandmother."

"They had a ton of fun, judging from the journal." Sara smiled. "Listen, I'll tell you what. Let's have our own book club, okay? None of my people are readers."

"I read," Alex said mildly and pointed at his book.

"But you only read hardcore thrillers and military novels. I'd love to have someone to talk to about my books. Romance and women's fiction and mysteries."

"Yeah, that's not going to be me." Alex looked at Hannah. "You?"

"Yes. I'd like that." Hannah smiled. "It's sweet that our grandmothers had a book club. Let's have another one. I'd like that."

Sara nodded, almost taken aback by how easy it was to connect to Hannah. Not many people got Sara. They quickly brushed her off as too much work, as too annoying and too nosy. But Sara was just so *bored.* Bored with her spreadsheets, bored with cooking the same handful of dishes her family liked to eat, bored with grocery shopping and chauffeuring teenagers and seniors, and bored with Andy's endless complaints about his job situation.

"Me too," Sara said, the words coming slowly. "I'd like that too, Hannah."

"But I have to buy my book," Hannah insisted.

"It's on the house." Alex crossed his arms.

Sara smiled. "How about I buy this one, and you can pick and buy next time?"

"Okay." Hannah nodded and tried to pick up her credit card. But her fingernails were freshly chewed to the quick. Finally, Alex picked it up and handed it to Hannah. She smiled an apology. "To be honest, I still don't know if this card still works."

"Do you know where the grocery store is?" Sara asked.

"There used to be a little Mom and Pop store around the corner," Hannah said. "Is that still there?"

"It is, but it's quite eclectic now," Sara said. "It's a good option for when you need specialty jams or fair-trade chocolate. There's a real supermarket in Pebble Beach. Best to stock up baseline supplies there."

"I go to the Mom and Pop store, and it's fine," Alex said. "Not everyone shops for a big family, Sara."

"That's true too," Sara admitted cheerfully. "Anyways, Hannah, here's my number." She pulled out the law firm's card and held it out. "If you call there, you'll get me on the phone. Let me know when you want to meet for our first book club meeting. I suggest the café on Mendocino Island. Or here, in the bookstore. We can push two chairs together and bring our own coffee."

"There's no coffee allowed in the store," Alex said stonily.

"You have coffee in the store all the time." Sara threw him a stern look.

Smiling, Hannah took the card and nodded. "I'll get settled, and then I'll call you."

"Read the first chapter too, if you can." Sara picked up her bag again. "I just started too. I'll wait for you before I read more."

"Thank you." Hannah tucked the card into her jeans pocket.

"Let me know if you need anything," Sara said. She really had to get back to work. "You too, Alex." She left before he could deny ever needing anything, and a few steps later, she was out of the store and hurrying along the sunny sidewalk back to the firm. She only stopped to buy a cheese croissant and a chocolate-walnut muffin.

Her mind, always running on a hamster wheel, was going over everything that had just happened.

Come to think of it, Sara did know another woman whose grandmother had been part of the club. Her name was Beth, and it was possible that she also still enjoyed reading books. Sara and Beth were out of touch during the pandemic. It had been a shock when Sara randomly spotted Beth's husband's obituary in the local newspaper. She'd sent a card but never heard back from Beth. Since that card, they had not been in contact.

"Maybe I'll ask Beth if she wants to join the book club," she whispered to herself as she pulled open the door to the small white house that housed Sterling Law. "Yes. Maybe I'll call Beth and see what she's up to."

CHAPTER 6

The door to the bookstore closed behind Sara, and Hannah, clutching her book like a lifeline, turned back to the bookseller's son.

"She's nice, even if she talks too fast," Alex said after a moment of looking back.

"I actually do remember Sara," Hannah said. "I think it's lovely that I can walk into this town and still know people."

"You remember her but not me?" He raised a dissatisfied eyebrow.

"Sorry." She smiled. She wished she could remember Alex. How had he never been in the store when she came on the weekend with her mother to buy books? Or maybe he had been in the store, and she'd been too focused on picking out the new book to take notice.

"You know..." With a put-upon sigh, Alex leaned back in his chair and crossed his hands behind his head. "Sara's right. Your husband can't just say the house is his. Even if his name is the only one on the deed."

Hannah had no idea what the divorce law was in California because it had never occurred to her to look it up. And frankly, she still didn't want to do it. She didn't want a divorce. She wanted the old Evan back, and the new beachside life they'd dreamed about.

"It's getting late," she said, suddenly keenly aware of Alex's piercing blue gaze holding hers. "I should clean up a bit more."

He nodded. "Sorry about that."

"It's not at all messy. Just a little dusty. And there's beach sand on the floor. I'm sure it'll scratch the wood floors."

"There's a washer and dryer in the back," he said and pointed a thumb over his shoulder. "Feel free to use them if you want to wash the bed sheets. If there are sheets."

"There are sheets," she confirmed. "They smell nice."

"Aha."

The eye pierced even more, enough to make Hannah flush. "So...thanks for the broom and the book." She also needed a dustpan, but she felt like she had asked more than enough of the man. "Thanks very much, Alex. I really appreciate you letting me stay."

He dropped his arms and picked up his book. "Yup. No worries." The blue eye fixed on the page but didn't move.

Hannah nodded and left the way she'd come, through the front door. Invading Alex's space behind the counter would be the shorter route to the apartment, but it seemed too personal.

Hannah went upstairs into the small apartment. Again it struck her that, like the bookstore below, the bedroom studio exuded a cozy air of safety and worn-in comfort. The bedroom half of the large room had a window out on the sea, and the living room part had one looking out on the sleepy, sun-drenched street. Sitting in one of the two armchairs felt like getting hugged and made it easy to see when someone was going to pay the bookstore a visit.

Hannah put the book on the coffee table and threw open the windows to let in the bright, fresh sea breeze. When sun and air flooded the little apartment, she began wiping the ledges and sills and shelves, shook out the white curtains so the breeze could carry the dust out over the ocean, and brushed the sand and salt off the windows. Then she swept the floors, using a sheet of an old newspaper as a dusting pan.

Cleaning felt good; it took her mind off Evan and the divorce.

Hannah scrubbed out the sink and then checked the cabinet. There were two pots, one big, one small, and she quickly washed the dust off them, then did the same for two plates, a small set of silverware, five glasses, and an old copper kettle. Following an impulse, she ran outside, across the street and onto the meadow that looked out on the sea. All afternoon, the fragrance of wildflowers blooming in full sun had drifted through the window and tempted her. She picked a handful of beach daisies and sea tuft and lupines for the apartment. It didn't take long to arrange the wildflowers in two of the glasses. One, she put on the nightstand, and the other, on the wooden coffee table.

When the apartment was sparkling clean, Hannah gathered the towels from the kitchen and the bathroom and pulled off the sheets, fluffing the stripped pillow and duvet and hanging them to air out the alley window.

Balling the linen up in her arms, she carried them back downstairs and tossed them in the washer. There was detergent on a shelf, so she used that. When the machine started whizzing and whirring, she gathered her courage and peeked into the store to let Alex know the noise was coming from her doing the laundry.

But the bookseller was gone. The stool behind the counter stood empty. Suddenly lonely, Hannah checked her phone. Time had flown, and to her surprise, it was almost five in the afternoon. She needed to buy her dinner, or the small market was going to close and she'd go hungry for the night.

In her mind, Hannah had pictured this first dinner back in Mendocino Beach a hundred times.

Maybe a picnic on the beach, smiling at her husband while the light of a small fire flickered over aged cheese and artisanal bread, grapes, Italian salami and olives. Or the two of them at a small, romantic restaurant in town, ordering spaghetti Bolognese, red wine, maybe tiramisu for dessert. Or maybe in the still-empty house, looking out at a sea of liquid gold and fire, sharing a roast chicken from the market, mac-and-cheese from a box, a simple green salad.

With Evan. Always, the image had included her husband. He'd been there with her, the two of them in love again, the way they had been when they first started dating.

Trying hard to wipe the painful images of those romantic dinners from her mind, Hannah hurried to find the small grocery store at the corner. She almost walked past it because the sign announcing this to be the Merman's Market was overgrown, hidden behind a curtain of tumbling yellow roses. But when she pushed against the brass knob of the door, it opened easily enough.

Hannah strolled through the store that smelled of fresh bread and parsley, sweet apples and the dill pickles in a barrel by the dairy counter. She grabbed a loaf of baguette bread, a chunk of brie, and two of the red-cheeked apples.

"Is that all you need today, honey?" The octogenarian lady at the register—as plump and round as a dumpling—looked at Hannah over her reading glasses as she put the groceries in a paper bag.

"Yes, that's all. Thank you." Hannah handed her the credit card and nervously watched as the lady ran it. There seemed to be no problem with the charge. Quietly exhaling a secret sigh of relief, Hannah took the card and tucked it back in her wallet.

At least Evan hadn't decided that the money in the bank account was his, too.

Hannah signed the slip, her lips pressed together, thanked the lady, took her bag, and left.

On the way back, she suddenly and without warning burst into tears. Drop after drop rolled down her cheeks, and though she kept wiping them away, they also kept coming.

Crying but determined to calm down before she returned to the studio and maybe ran into Alex or an unsuspecting bookstore patron, Hannah took a left and walked toward the harbor. Back in the day, there used to be an old stone wall that shielded the harbor from flood waves. And if Hannah knew one thing, then it was that unlike husbands, old sea walls had a habit of sticking around forever and ever.

CHAPTER 7

O f course the seawall was still there. And finally, the images of Evan, and the romantic dinners that weren't to be, and the house she'd lost receded like a timid tide.

Instead, memories of Mom and Hannah returned. On Market Day, the two of them had often stopped on the way home to sit on the warm fieldstones. They'd counted the fishing boats bobbing on the water and licked penny ice cream or sampled whatever they'd bought at the farmers market.

Hannah sat down, allowing the warmth of the old wall and the happy memories to calm her unsettled, aching heart. Still sniffling, she pulled out the loaf of bread and twisted off a small chunk. It was sourdough bread, a bit sweet, a bit tangy, with a perfectly crisp crust and fluffy inside. She chewed slowly, wiping her face until the pain softened and the rose-colored rays of the evening sun dried up the last tears.

For a while she sat, watching the waves that crested far out in the ocean before, tamed and limpid like sleepy kittens, they rolled in to lap at the nearby town beach as if the golden sand was made of strawberries and cream. White and gray gulls screamed as they circled and swooped over colorful fishing boats that brought home fresh catches. Closer than the gulls and the waves, near Hannah's feet, were fat, fuzzy bumble bees that dipped in and out of the velvet petals of California poppies that grew along the old, gray seawall. The air smelled of the sun-warmed field stones and fresh bread. Now and then, Hannah caught a whiff of the diesel fuel that propelled the fishing vessel toward land.

"Hey. Hi." Another woman had come up behind Hannah to sit on the stone wall.

"Hi." Hannah turned and shaded her eyes to see the woman.

She was near Hannah's age, maybe a bit older, wore flowy linen pants and matching tunic, and held a towering ice cream in her hand. The woman pointed at the wall beside Hannah. "Is it okay if I sit down?"

"Yes, of course." Hannah pulled her bag closer even though there was plenty of space.

The woman smiled and nodded thanks, then climbed over the wall and sat, balancing her scoops of chocolate and strawberry that were topped with cream and sprinkled with what looked and smelled like roasted hazelnuts.

"That looks delicious," Hannah said just to be friendly.

"It's the best. You *have* to try it. I got it at the Ice Creamery. It's behind the Merman's Market." The woman nodded at Hannah's bag. The brown paper had the store's pretty logo of a shell wreath with the market's loopy initials printed on it. "Are you visiting or local?"

"I used to live here." Hannah fudged over the story of her sad day. "I'm not sure how long I'll stay."

"Mh-mm." The woman was busy making sure the ice cream didn't melt over her hands. "Hey, if you want one, they're closing in ten minutes." She smiled an apology. "I always feel bad eating ice cream alone."

"Oh." Hannah was about to tell her not to feel bad but stopped herself. She also didn't enjoy eating ice cream by herself. It was a social thing, especially when you were sitting on the sea wall. "You know, I think I will get one." She smiled and stood, brushing the crumbs of her taste of the sourdough bread off her T-shirt.

The woman smiled back. "Leave your things. I'll watch your bag."

Hannah hurried up the street. Suddenly, she *wanted* that ice cream. The last crying spell had left her parched and hungry for something sweet and creamy and comforting. She wandered through the narrow streets, looking for the Ice Creamery and dodging climbing roses and waving lupines. It was good to know that whatever Evan did, there was still ice cream... There still were seawalls and golden beaches. And there was the kindness of strangers.

Alex had given her a place to stay. Sara had invited her to start a book club. And the woman on the seawall wanted to share an ice cream moment by the sea.

The ice cream store was already shutting down when she finally found it. Thinking she was too late, she turned away. But the young man spotted her and called her over, happy to let Hannah have the last ice cream of the day and promising to make her scoop of salted caramel swirl extra-extra big. Not only did he keep his promise, but he topped the ice generously and unprompted with chopped chocolate nuts, salty toffee bits, a spoonful of hot fudge sauce, and all the whipped cream that was left.

Hannah laughed as she reached for the warm waffle cone with its teetering load. "Thank you," she said and handed over her card. "I need this."

The guy behind the counter smiled and handed it back. "Ciao, bella," he said and winked. "Today, beauty pays. Enjoy."

Hannah couldn't help but smile on her way back. Now that she had breached the big forty, it wasn't every day that her looks got her an ice cream.

When she returned, the woman was still on the sea wall, eating her ice cream and watching the ocean, Hannah's grocery bag beside her. Hannah sat down in her old spot and tasted her caramel swirl. "Mh-mm. I'm glad I listened to you. It tastes amazing."

The woman smiled. "Doesn't it? I always have one when I come to Mendocino Beach."

"I see why." Hannah turned back to the sea, eating the creamy ice that was sweet and salty and chocolatey, letting the toasted nuts and crunchy toffee claim her attention. The sun dropped lower and lower toward the flaming sea that waited for her good night kiss.

When Hannah was done with her treat, it was time to return to her little apartment. She still had to dry the towels and sheets and put them on the bed. Brushing the latest round of crumbs off her jeans, she tried to stay in the beautiful moment. It was better than thinking about the coming night. The quiet and dark, she knew, would find her lonely and confused.

Maybe she would call Evan. Maybe he had changed his mind. It couldn't have been more than a spur-of-the-moment thing, brought on by stress. But even if he asked her to come back—she'd stay the night. She needed to make sure he knew not to treat her like that ever again.

"I'm sorry." When Hannah looked up, the woman beside her was smiling at her. "I don't usually bother strangers. But I was wondering...you wouldn't be Hannah Banner, would you?"

"I am," Hannah said, surprised. "Do we know each other?"

CHAPTER 8

"My name is Elizabeth Thompson," the woman said. "Beth Thompson? I was a couple of grades above you in school."

Once again, Hannah didn't recognize the face or the name. "I'm sorry," she said helplessly. "I'm afraid..."

"No worries." Beth smiled her quiet smile. "It's a very long time ago. I used to envy your blue eyes and brown curls. That's why I remember you. I always wanted curls like yours. My entire life." She chuckled. "And you know what? I still want them. Your hair is just stunning."

"Thank you." Hannah blinked. "Yours is too. I love the silver."

Beth's hair was still dark, but strands of silver glittered like diamonds in the light of the sinking sun. "Thanks," Beth said. "I decided to go gray after my husband died in the pandemic. The transition wasn't easy."

Hannah wasn't sure whether Beth was talking about the demarcation line or the death of her husband. "I'm sure," she murmured awkwardly. "I'm so sorry about your husband."

Beth took an audible breath. "My friend Sara called me earlier," she said. "In fact, she told me Hannah Banner was in town. I thought it was you when I saw you sitting here. Is it true that the two of you have started a book club?"

"Yes, we have, sort of." Hannah smiled. She'd forgotten how quickly news spread in a town as small as Mendocino Beach. "Our first book is a mystery." She pulled the book out of her purse and handed it to Beth.

"Ooh." Beth took it and, interested, flipped through the pages. "I love mysteries."

Hannah hesitated for a moment but then plunged ahead. If Sara had told Beth about the book club, surely, she wouldn't mind if Beth joined them. "Would you like to join the book club?" she asked. "We'll meet in a coffee place or maybe the bookstore if it's okay with the owner."

Smiling, Beth looked up. "I would love to come. I have to admit that Sara already asked, and I said yes. I hoped you wouldn't mind." Beth handed the book back. "I even have a copy of the book at home. I have a TBR stack a mile long hogging my bedside table. I'm sure I've seen it somewhere in there."

"Great!" Hannah slipped the book back into her purse, happy with the development. Quiet and collected, Beth would be the perfect counterpart to Sara's wild energy.

"Sara said that our grandmothers were in a book club." Beth looked out at the ocean. "I think that's why she called to tell me about the book club."

"Really?" Hannah straightened her back.

Beth nodded. "To be honest, Sara's call came quite out of the blue. I think she avoided me after my husband died. A lot of people did."

"And *I* thought," Sara's voice suddenly rang out behind them, "that *you* ghosted *me*, Beth." She put a hand on Beth's shoulder and climbed over the wall to sit between Beth and Hannah. "Because you never got in touch after the note I sent."

"*You* didn't get in touch," Beth pointed out, but like Sara, she was smiling, a smile that reached her eyes.

"So nobody ghosted anyone!" Hannah dared throw in. "Sounds like a misunderstanding, maybe?"

Beth lightly elbowed Sara, barely touching her ribs. "I was truly out of it, Sara. I probably did ghost you while feeling sorry for myself. Sorry if I did."

"Well, now that you said it... I really should've tried harder to be there for you. But I honestly wasn't sure what to do. I didn't want to bother you."

"Nobody knows what to do." Beth looked down at her hands. "I still don't know what to do without Ben."

"Hannah's hubby here told her he wants a divorce today." Now it was Sara who lightly touched her elbow to Hannah's arm. "How are you holding up, honey pie?"

Hannah took a deep breath. "I'm worried about tonight!" it broke from her. "I don't think I'll sleep a wink. I was hoping he would call me to tell me this is all a huge mistake. But he hasn't gotten in touch at all! He only texted me the number for the moving truck with my books. I really need to call him."

Sara weaved her head. "If you call, please do me a favor and record everything, will you?"

Hannah tucked her chin. "Why? Do you want to listen to it?"

"No, I really don't." Sara put her hand on both Hannah's and Beth's shoulders as she rose and climbed back over the wall on the street. "But record the call and keep the recording somewhere safe, all right? Your lawyer might be able to use it."

"But I still don't want a lawyer," Hannah said, her stomach dropping at the thought.

"I know. I know." Sara patted Hannah reassuringly. "Do it anyway."

"Where are you going?" Beth looked over her shoulder at Sara. "Can't you stay a bit longer? We could talk about the book club."

Sara sighed. "If only. But I have to go home and come up with something to cook. Something yummy that a depressed man, two spoiled teenagers, and four picky seniors will enjoy. The list of ingredients I can't use is as long as my arm. Wish me luck."

"Good luck," Hannah and Beth said at the same time. Sara hurried off, and Beth rose as well. "Call your husband," she advised Hannah. "See if you can't get him to talk about his feelings. New beginnings can be scary. Maybe he really is just overreacting."

"I think I will." She waved Beth good night, and her new acquaintance left. Hannah pulled out her phone and glanced at the bars. There was still enough battery left for a long talk.

Hannah's finger hovered over her phone, ready to dial her husband's number.

But something in her was too afraid to do it.

What if he said he truly was serious about the divorce?

What would she do then? She couldn't live over the bookstore forever.

Slowly, Hannah let the phone sink again and closed her eyes. She couldn't face any more unfair accusations. Or the thought that she still hadn't seen the inside of her beloved childhood home.

Was Evan making himself dinner in her mother's kitchen right now, congratulating himself on getting rid of a wife who was not rich and no longer pretty?

For the first time, a feeling of defiance rose in her chest.

Hannah grabbed her bag and purse and stood, shaking the sand from the seawall from her jeans.

She would go into her little studio and eat bread and cheese and a glass of water before going to bed and sleeping as best she could. If she couldn't sleep, she would open the window and look at the moon and the stars and listen to the sea's lullaby. Tomorrow, she would have breakfast at the cute bakery she'd spotted near the ice cream shop. Once she was done with her coffee and her croissant, once she had taken care of her body and soul, *then* she would call Evan.

She sighed.

It wasn't much of a plan, but it was a plan.

Hannah climbed over the wall. The sun had dipped into the water, the last rays swimming on the waves, and the air was soft and warm.

It was the blue hour, the time of stories and books and dreams and her favorite time of the day. She put her head back in her neck. High above, in the velvety plum evening sky, the first stars started to twinkle like promises and tears and diamonds on the queen's best dress.

CHAPTER 9

B eth looked at the menu card of the small pizzeria. Tonight of all nights, she had planned to
make dinner at home. But now, in the beauty of
the blue hour, she found herself unwilling to leave
Mendocino Beach.

Her house was outside of town. To be fair, it was
a beautiful house, larger than most out here and
surrounded by acres of meadows that twinkled and
sparkled with fireflies at night. Her husband had been
an architect, and he'd designed the house himself.

Beth had never understood how she, of all women,
had been so lucky to find her soul mate. She hadn't
even believed in true love and soul mates. But like
a gift from heaven, she had received this particular
blessing when she met Ben.

Then, a year ago to the day, he'd died of cancer.
His death left a rent in her heart that no amount of
grieving, therapy, or soul food seemed to patch.

She'd meant to go home and cook his favorite dish,
eggplant Parmesan, set the table for him and herself
both, and then allow herself to cry as much as she
wanted. Again.

But the young night was as soft and warm as velvet. Despite the sad anniversary, Beth didn't want to cry into her eggplant Parmesan. She wanted a pizza and a glass of red wine.

Guiltily, she eyed the posted menu in the glow of a streetlamp. She'd promised to honor Ben's memory, always. But making eggplant Parmesan took a long time, and despite the ice cream earlier she was really hungry, and the fragrant scent of home-cooked marinara and garlic roasting in sizzling olive oil wrapped temptingly around her like a soft, comfortable scarf.

Her therapist would be delighted if she chose the pizza.

And Ben?

Beth took a deep breath and squared her shoulders. Then she put a hand on the handle of polished olive-tree wood and opened the door.

Outside, the dark was full of mystery and mystique. But inside the restaurant, the light was golden warm, and the air was heavy with delicious, savory scents, alive with the murmur of low conversation and laughter, and cheery with the flicker of candles on red-checkered tablecloths.

Beth had forgotten how to go places by herself. She'd not been out for dinner since Ben died, and hardly ever alone. In fact, she was a little worried. Would people stare? Figure she was a widow and pity her? Throw her out?

A server came over to where she, feeling helpless, stood near the entrance. "Good evening. Table for one?" He picked up a single menu and held it up in question.

She smiled, glad he hadn't asked if she belonged to a party. "Yes," she said humbly. "Thank you."

"You came at the right moment." He winked at her. "I just had a table open by the window. If you don't mind that I still need to clear it?"

"No, of course not. A table by the window would be lovely." She followed him past other tables full of couples and friends enjoying dinner together.

"Here we go." He put the menu down. There were still bowls and platters on the table, but the used plates and glasses had already been taken away.

"Thank you." She nodded and sat, glad she'd been brave and come in. It really was a good table, looking out at the sea. It was too dark already to see the ocean, but every now and then, she could see a wave crest white against the rocky cliff beyond the bluff. When she smiled, he pulled out a chair.

Her server threw her an appraising glance as he stacked the bowls and platters. "A glass of wine, certainly. I recommend a smooth red with blunted tannins and a texture as elegant and classy as you are, belladonna. Usually, I'd say Pinot Noir. But no..." Lifting the dishes, he straightened, regarding her thoughtfully. "Not tonight. Maybe the Malbec. Its flavor of blackberry, dark summer plum, and warm spice is like a comforting embrace."

Confused, Beth lowered her chin. How did he know she needed comforting? "Okay, yes please," she said politely. She couldn't remember what wines Ben used to like. Travel, wine, and good food had been his expertise, not hers. She'd been the partner who bought their books and kept track of movie channel subscriptions and changed the flowers in the vases when they wilted.

It didn't take long for the server to come back and bring her a long-stemmed glass of deep red wine. She ordered her frutti di mare pizza and, when she was alone again, lifted the wine glass to her lips. "To you, my love," she breathed, closed her eyes, and drank.

As promised, the wine teetered between summer and fall, blackberries and plum and cinnamon. Also as promised, it soothed her. She relaxed into her chair, remembering how she'd met Ben for the first time. She'd been browsing for a beach romance in the bookstore, and he'd been looking for Homer's Odyssey. He asked her out for a coffee, and the rest was love and history.

She took another sip.

Truly history. It was over. Ben was gone. And she was still left.

"Here you go, ma'am." A new server set a woven basket of fragrant, perfectly toasted rosemary focaccia on her table. "Another glass of wine?"

"Please." Beth slid her empty glass over the checkered tablecloth. The server took it and left. She looked over her shoulder, wondering what had happened to the first server, the one who'd called her belladonna, pretty woman, and recommended the Malbec. After a moment of searching, she spotted him standing behind the counter, talking with yet another server.

He looked Italian, she decided, with his angled jaw and straight Roman nose, brown eyes and dark wavy hair that just showed the first threads of silver at the temples. Like the other staff, he was wearing a crisp white button-down shirt rolled up at the sleeves, a black vest, jeans, and a long black apron tied around the waist.

As if he'd noticed her gaze, he suddenly turned his head and glanced at her. Their eyes met, and Beth quickly looked away. She picked up a chunk of focaccia, just so he didn't think she needed anything. She didn't. And the restaurant was too busy for unnecessary trips.

Idly, she bit into the bread. The crisp crust hid a soft and pillowy inside that was fragrant with rosemary and olive oil. A little salty, but also a bit sweet. She popped the rest into her mouth and reached for another piece just as her second glass of wine arrived.

Beth looked up, her mouth stuffed full of toasted bread, her lips shiny with olive oil. It was the first server again, the one who knew what wine she needed. Quickly, she held a hand in front of her mouth. "Thank you very much," she mumbled, trying not to spit breadcrumbs.

With a practiced movement, he set down the new glass. "It is no longer Malbec."

"It isn't?" Disappointed, Beth looked at the glass.

"It's the Merlot," the server remarked casually, his lips shaping into a faint smile. "You'll find it has delightful notes of summer cherries, with a subtle hint of chocolate. A sweet temper, as gentle as the night." His gaze lingered briefly on her face, a gentle warmth in his eyes, before he continued. "I thought you might enjoy it." With a small nod, he turned away.

Beth stopped chewing and turned to look after him. Her spidey sense was tingling. First the belladonna, now the sweet temper. She shook her head and swallowed her bread. Nonsense. Nobody flirted with a middle-aged widow who was getting a bit pudgy around the middle, least of all a charming, good-looking man like him. Beth knew perfectly well that at her age, she was practically invisible to men.

She glanced down to make sure none of the buttons of her blouse had popped off. Then she tried the new wine. Again, it was just as he'd promised. Summer fruit and a hint of chocolate, a little bit sweet but not too much. She drank the wine much too quickly and nodded at the next passing server, who brought her one more glass.

Beth could feel her thoughts starting to slow and blood warm her cheeks. It felt nice, but also a bit dangerous. She was glad when her pizza arrived soon after the third glass of wine.

It was larger than she'd expected; the hot pizza stone took up half the table. The pizza itself looked like a work of art with its thin, golden crust, and when Beth inhaled, the tantalizing scent of the seafood mingled with the earthy aroma of freshly baked dough.

Eagerly, Beth pulled a luscious slice on her plate and bit into it. The crust was perfectly thin and crispy, with just the right amount of chewiness around the edges. It was brushed with a light coating of garlic-infused olive oil that added a subtle depth of flavor to each bite and carried a medley of flavorful shrimp, tender calamari, flaky crab meat, and succulent mussels, all nestled in a scattering of roast baby clams.

"Is it good?" The first server stopped by again.

And again, Beth needed to hide her chewing lips behind a coy hand. "Yes," she mumbled happily. "It is absolutely delicious."

He nodded, looking satisfied. "My father had a pizza shop on Via dei Serpenti."

She tilted her head and swallowed, dropping the hand. She seemed to remember the name. Maybe Ben had mentioned it. "Isn't that in Rome?"

"Yes." He smiled. "That is in Rome." He hurried on, back to the counter where he started pouring brandy into wide-bellied glasses.

Beth had eaten almost a quarter of the pizza when it occurred to her that not all servers here would have fathers with pizzerias in Rome, on a street famous for its restaurants. Again she glanced at the counter.

Her Roman server leaned against a shelf behind the bar, his arms crossed, locking eyes with her. Emboldened by the wine and good food, Beth smiled at him. He didn't return the smile as a man looking like a blond surfer from Malibu asked him a question. The server answered, gesturing with his hands as he spoke, and Malibu vanished back into the kitchen.

Beth ate another slice, and another, and one more, eating her way from shrimp to mussel to calamari while dreamily watching for white tufts on the dark ocean and smiling at the conversations at other tables.

Finally, feeling stuffed to the brim, she reluctantly pushed away her plate and leaned back to sip her wine. As if the pizza had kept the memories at bay and her protection was now gone, she remembered what day it was.

In the midst of enjoying wine and plump shrimp, she had completely forgotten about Ben.

A cold, hard wave of guilt washed over her. Not a gentle kitten lick, but a real crusher.

Gasping, Beth set down her empty wine glass. What in heaven was she doing? She was supposed to be at home, making Ben's eggplant Parmesan!

"You should not have another glass," the Roman server said gently, appearing out of nowhere beside her, and picked up the empty wine glass. "For a woman like you, so sad and beautiful, three is good."

She looked up at him, confused. "The check, please."

"Ah." His gaze fell on the ravished pizza. "And would you like a doggy-pack for the rest?"

Despite her emotional state, Beth had to smile. "A doggy bag? No, thank you. It was delicious fresh out of the oven, and that's how I'd like to remember it."

Respect glimmered in his dark eyes. "That is good," he said. "That means you'll come back to eat again."

Yes, she wanted to say. *It was the best food I've had in a year. Of course I'll come back.*

But instead her lips moved without forming the words, as if she were drunk.

"No dessert? Tiramisu?" He picked up her pizza with his free hand, not looking at her.

"No thank you," she finally managed to say. "Just the check, please."

CHAPTER 10

The squawk of a gull woke Hannah. Sleepily, she blinked into the sun that shone through the open window onto her face. When she remembered where she was, and why, Hannah sighed and turned on her side to look out the window at the glistening sea. The soft pillow under her head shifted with the cozy crackle of down feathers, and the cool sea breeze from the open window caressed her face as she snuggled into a comfortable position.

The night before, Evan hadn't answered the phone. He still wanted a divorce, then. He still wanted the house.

And Hannah was *starving*.

With a low growl, Hannah pushed the thick feather duvet off. The scent of freshly washed linen rose around her, and the oversized striped pajama top brushed over her knees as she set her bare feet on the floor. "Oops," she murmured and smoothed the crumpled top.

Last night, when she had finally finished putting the clean linen back on the bed, she couldn't get herself to sleep in the sweaty, dusty T-shirt she'd been wearing all day. Sleeping naked seemed too risky. It was a stranger's apartment after all, and Hannah felt anything but sensual.

After a few minutes of pondering this new aggravation, she'd decided it was okay to rummage through the old cedar closet. To her relief, there'd been old men's clothes in it, including two neatly folded pajamas. One of the button-down tops easily counted as a nightgown, and when she'd pulled it on, she was pleasantly surprised to find it smelled not of dust and mothballs but of lavender and the wardrobe's red cedar wood.

She had taken a quick shower in the tiny avocado-green bathroom, and then she'd slipped into the crisp pajama top and cuddled into the soft, cozy bed. After a few minutes, she got back up and padded barefoot across the dark room to open the window before diving back into her warm bed.

There were moments when tears flowed down Hannah's cheeks. There were moments when her heart widened at the beauty of the bright moon and sparkling stars and the fragrance of the wildflowers that the breeze carried inside. There were moments when she cursed her husband and moments when she missed him, moments when the rushing of the sea comforted her and moments when her head and heart ached with fear for the future. And in between all these moments, somehow, sometime, she had fallen asleep.

Now, Hannah opened the door to her little apartment. Golden sunlight streamed inside, and rubbing her arms to warm them, she stepped out on the landing.

The last streaks of fog still slunk around the bottom of the staircase, but it was a beautiful morning, even for Mendocino. The sun would soon burn the last of the cool mist of the night.

When she heard a door open below, Hannah stood on tiptoes and peeked over the railing.

"Morning." Alex blinked up at her, his hair disheveled and his muscular upper body exposed. The pajama pants he wore matched her top perfectly. He ran a hand through his hair and adjusted the eye patch. "Are you wearing my PJs?"

"Uh." Hannah considered hopping back inside, but it was too late. She thrust a thumb over her shoulder. "I found them in the closet. I didn't think they were yours."

"Ah. Yeah, I put some clothes up there when I moved in." He turned to look at the ocean.

"I'm sorry," she said awkwardly. "I should've asked, but I didn't want to bother you that late."

He waved the apology away. "No worries. Take what clothes you need. Just run them through the washer before you leave."

"Sure. I'll do that. Thanks very much." Relieved he wasn't annoyed, Hannah wondered how much Alex used the apartment himself. More than he let on?

Unbothered, he scratched his chin. "Do you want coffee?"

Her eyes widened. "Yes, please. If you don't mind."

When he looked up at her, shading his eye against the sun, he was grinning. "Hang on just a minute."

Hannah settled on the top step, waiting as the morning air grew warmer, carrying the shy notes of sea salt and fresh kelp, along with the scents of drying driftwood and flowering beach heather. She attempted to tame her tousled curls with her fingers, but they remained unruly, the corkscrew twists rebelling after a restless night of tossing and turning in the salty air. She resigned herself to untangling them later.

Before long, the door below thudded shut, and Alex emerged. He had thrown on a gray T-shirt and carried two steaming mugs. Slowly, he ascended the stairs and settled on the step below hers, offering her one of the mugs. "Here you go, ma'am," he murmured.

"Thank you, Alex," she said gratefully, wrapping her hands around the warm mug. "I would've come down. Isn't it painful to climb the stairs?"

"Not so much in the mornings," he replied, taking a sip and leaning back, his elbow resting close beside her feet, almost touching her leg.

The gesture felt strangely familiar, startling her. But then, she was wearing the top to his pajama bottoms. It all felt a bit forbidden.

And he smelled good, too. Of man-soap and after-shave, despite not having shaved. Maybe it was his deodorant.

Smiling, Hannah sipped her black coffee, surprised to find comfort in the bitter, unadulterated taste that pulled on her senses and demanded her attention. Lowering her mug, she said, "Hey, Alex?"

"What?" He kept his gaze fixed on the ocean.

"I really appreciate your help," she said from the bottom of her heart. "I want you to know that."

It took him a moment to respond. "It's all right, Hannah. No worries."

She smiled. "Not many people would help a stranger the way you do. I'll never forget it."

"Mh-mm." He took another drink, and for a while, they sat in silence. Then he spoke again. "I've lost a lot of friends in combat. Good men, all of them. It changed me." Slowly, he set his mug down. "Hold out a hand while you can, you know? It matters."

She pressed her lips together, fighting the urge to reach out and touch him. "Hold out a hand," she repeated quietly. "It does matter."

"So." He cleared his throat. "That husband of yours? What a douchebag."

Startled, Hannah straightened. "What?"

Alex rubbed a hand over his chin. "That man's a douchebag."

"He—what?" In her confusion, she laughed.

"Telling you to take the car and go away, after you've just arrived in town? I can't believe he did that. Why didn't he say something while you were still back home?"

Hannah swallowed as all that misery rushed back to her. "I know. I can't believe it either. But he's not really a *douchebag*."

"Let alone tell you *he's* going to live in your mother's house."

"Okay. So maybe he's a bit of a douchebag," Hannah admitted.

"And you're a doormat."

"I'm not a doormat! How dare you." She frowned.

"Then don't let him get away with it. Go tell him your opinion."

"*You* go tell him your opinion." Hannah drained her mug and rubbed both hands over her face. "It's not so easy after you've been married for ten years. You wouldn't understand."

"Maybe I do, maybe I don't. I was married for a year before she left," Alex said. "And she cleaned me out good when she did."

"Oh. Shoot, Alex. Wait. Does that mean...you're a doormat too?" Hannah grinned.

"Nah." With a sigh, he grabbed the railing and pulled himself up. "I gave her everything she wanted so she wouldn't come back. Once I'm done, I'm done." He eyed her. "How about you?"

"I'm not done," she said quietly. "I still want him back. I'll fight for my marriage."

"Yeah." He picked up the empty mugs and turned, slowly climbing down the stairs while leaning heavily on the railing. "For a while, that's what I thought I'd do too. I guess a lot of us do, at first."

"Ten years is longer than one year. It's different."

"Well, good luck. I'll see you later."

"See you later," Hannah called after him.

At the bottom of the stairs, he looked back up, squinting through the gaps in the boards. "Hey, Hannah. I meant to ask...what is it you do?"

She leaned to see him through the wooden slats. "You mean for a job?"

"Yeah."

"I'm a librarian, Mr. Bookstore Owner." She smiled. "I muck around with board books and read stories to kids and seniors."

"Of course you do." He shook his head as he walked back inside.

A gull landed beside her and screamed, opening his orange beak wide.

"Did you wake me up this morning?" Hannah shaded her eyes to look at him. "Yeah? Then I'll call you Henry. You can be my alarm clock."

Henry lifted his wing to inhale and screamed.

"I should go get breakfast? I mean, if you insist." Hannah rose and shook her curls back. Having coffee with Alex had cheered her up. "And right after breakfast, I'll call Evan and tell him what I think about his divorce."

Henry made a croaking sound, spread his wings dramatically, and flew away.

CHAPTER 11

"Hey! Hannah! Wait for me!"

Hannah stopped and turned, looking up the sun-drenched street. It took her a moment to spot the caller among all the people walking toward the harbor, and she had to sidestep a few passersby as she waited for her new book club friend. "Good morning, Sara."

"Fancy meeting you here!" Smiling, Sara caught up with Hannah, swinging a grocery net in her hand. "I didn't know you were going to the farmers market too!"

Impulsively, Hannah hugged the other woman. "Actually, I was going to the bakery next to the ice cream store. I haven't had breakfast yet."

"Ah, you can go there any old day. Come with me—they have so many great baking stands at the market! We can eat together. I haven't had breakfast either."

"Sure." Hannah smiled. "I'm not making you late for work?"

"It's all right. Thank goodness for the glamorous life of a paralegal assistant with flexible hours." Sara chuckled. "Grocery shopping by day, saving the world by night." She patted the back pocket of her pants. "Meet my trusty sidekick: the work phone." With a wink, she added, "Never leaves my side, not even at the vegetable stand. As long as I take our clients' calls, my boss won't fire me."

"Well, then let's go find something to eat!" Hannah fell into step behind Sara as they made their way down to the town's quaint harbor. She couldn't help but feel a rush of nostalgia as they approached the farmers market she and her mother remembered so fondly.

Back then, there had been pop-up tables with home-made breads and jams, veggies so fresh they still had moist, black soil clinging to the roots, and fish with scales and eyes as bright as the ocean. The rickety tables of the eighties were gone, but pretty, multi-tiered stands and white canvas tents lined the busy aisles.

"There's a German baker who makes fantastic cinnamon buns." Sara unceremoniously hooked her arm under Hannah's. "Have you started the book yet?"

"No," Hannah admitted, her nose lifted slightly in the air to catch every tantalizing scent wafting from the stands. "I was pretty upset about the divorce last night."

Sara patted her hand sympathetically. "Oh, I would be too. But you should read the first chapter. It pulls you right into the story, and then you forget about that beastly husband of yours."

"He's not beastly," Hannah said quickly. "I just don't know what's going on with him."

Sara glanced at her. "Maybe he's crying his eyes out right now, regretting every single word he said to you yesterday," she said, her voice unconvinced. "Look, that's the baker I told you about." She pointed, but then her work phone buzzed, and she pulled it out of her pocket with an apologetic glance at Hannah. "Oh goodness, sorry. I've got to take this."

"Sure." Hannah nodded. "I'll get us cinnamon buns." While Sara went to a quieter spot, Hannah joined the meandering line of customers. "Is this the end of the line?"

"Yes, it is." The woman in front of her shuffled to make space for her in the busy market aisle. Suddenly, she turned around. "Hannah! I thought I recognized the voice. It took me a second."

"Beth!" Hannah smiled. "I already met Sara, and now you're here too!"

Beth's smile looked a little forced, and she put a hand to her temple, rubbing it. "We're all here all the time, Hannah. Welcome back to life in a small town."

"Are you okay?" Hannah asked. "You look like you're in pain."

"I have a headache," Beth said. "I had one too many glasses of wine last night."

"Oh. Got it."

"Yeah." Beth shuffled forward as another customer finished their business. "I went to this little pizza place I'd never been to before, and..." She stopped talking and blinked. "And how are you? Did you talk with your husband?"

"He didn't answer the phone," Hannah said. She heard herself how lame it sounded. "I'm going to eat a bite and try again." They shuffled another step closer, and now Hannah could smell the brown sugar, the warm cinnamon, and the butter emanating from the soft, hot pastries displayed on the wooden shelf. The ladies running the stand bagged them as quickly as they could, replenishing the supply from a small van. Smoke curled from a stove pipe, telling Hannah that the van had an oven.

"Are you worried?" Beth asked.

Hannah nodded. "I'm really worried. What if he just won't talk to me? He was so...so *weird* yesterday. I mean, we've been together for ten years and never even had a fight."

"Not a single one?" Beth sounded astonished. "In ten years of marriage, not a single fight?"

"No. Not a single one," Hannah confirmed. "I know it's not normal. But I always thought it was *good*."

The corners of Beth's mouth dropped as if she didn't agree. "I married the love of my life," she said. "And we fought. But we stuck it out and always made up again too. I couldn't imagine never having a fight. Or at least an argument?" She turned. "Hi. Five cinnamon buns and two elephant ears dipped in chocolate, please."

"I mean, we've had an argument," Hannah murmured, just because she was embarrassed to admit how blind she'd been to the reality of her relationship. But they hadn't had arguments either. Sometimes, Evan would leave the house and not come back for a night. But he'd always be friendly the next day, just as if nothing had happened. And the nights alone always gave Hannah a fright, if she was honest. She felt abandoned, and left behind, and less-than. She couldn't stand the feeling, so she tried to avoid topics that might make Evan uncomfortable.

If she needed anything, she texted him. And if he ignored the text, she knew he didn't agree or didn't want to do what she asked. She adjusted to that too, just as if he'd told her what he needed.

But now, seemingly out of the blue, Evan wanted a divorce. Maybe the peace Hannah had sought so much had been toxic after all. Maybe now, they truly did need to talk about the uncomfortable bit.

But how, if Evan either left or didn't answer the phone in the first place?

"Two cinnamon buns, please," Hannah said when it was her turn. The white-aproned woman put two hot, steaming buns into a paper bag for her, and Hannah handed over the credit card.

"Oh," the woman said. "We only take cash."

"I don't have cash. I'm sorry, I didn't know." Hannah awkwardly slipped her card back into her pocket.

"I got you." Beth, who'd been waiting for her, put a five-dollar bill on the counter.

"Thanks." The baker put the money into her box. "Next!"

Hannah took the bag and followed Beth. "I'm sorry," she said again. "You didn't have to do that."

"I know, but it's no problem." Beth smiled. "Where's Sara?"

Hannah turned to look for her new friend. There were more people milling about now between the pretty stands than when she'd arrived, with new ones entering the market every moment.

Something caught Hannah's eye. A flash of a smile, a glint of an eye, a mouth she knew.

A mouth she'd kissed for ten years.

Blood shot into her cheeks. Evan, in shirtsleeves and pressed khakis, was walking straight toward her. He hadn't spotted her yet among the people, and he looked happy and well-rested.

Hannah couldn't take her eyes off his smiling face. And when she finally regained command over her gaze, all she could do was stare at the woman on his arm.

Carrying a cheerful bouquet of beach daisies, she was in her late twenties. At the height of her beauty. Cornflower eyes, raven hair—and a hugely pregnant belly.

The woman was laughing up at Evan, clinging to his arm.

Clinging to Hannah's *husband's* arm.

"Hannah? There you are!" Sara called out, waving at her.

Evan's eyes flickered to Sara, and then to Hannah, opening wide. He stopped, almost causing the pregnant woman at his side to stumble. "What?" she asked in alarm.

"Evan?" Hannah's voice was as ashen and gray as her heart felt. "Who is that?"

Turning to her, the younger woman frowned. "Who are *you*? Evan? Who is she? Do you know her?"

Evan's chest rose and sank in a gargantuan sigh, and then he extricated the pregnant woman from his arm. Protectively, he stepped in front of her. "Hannah, I told you to go back to San Jose."

His words reached her through a dream-like layer of cotton in her ears. Fuzzily, she registered that Sara and Beth had come to stand at her sides like sentinels. "Are you the father of her baby?" Hannah asked in a whisper.

Evan held out a hand as if to make her stop talking, but Hannah only stared at it uncomprehendingly. "Yes," he finally said, defiance in his voice. "I meant to tell you, Hannah."

"You meant to tell me?" Hannah blinked. "How long...how long have you...and her..."

"Who *is* this, Evan?" The pregnant woman cradled her belly. "What's going on?"

"Four years," Evan said quietly, staring directly into Hannah's eyes. "Four years, Hannah. Four happy years."

"Happy?" The word felt like glue in her mouth. Her last four years with him hadn't been particularly happy. Just normal good. No, not even that. *Just* normal.

"Very happy." He sighed and held out a hand to the pregnant woman. Irritated, she took it and stepped beside him. "This is Allison. Allison, this is Hannah."

"Who in the world is Hannah?"

"His wife," Hannah said slowly. "We've been married for ten years."

"Are you serious?" Allison whisked her hand from Evan's. "You are *married?* You piece of—"

"Oh, no. Please, no." Bile rose in Hannah's throat. "I didn't know. I had no idea."

Her face blanching to the white of the daisies in her hand, Allison turned on her heel and strode in the opposite direction, pushing tourists out of the way.

"Alli!" Evan called after her. When he looked back at Hannah, his face was furious. She'd never seen him like that. "I'm about to be a *father*, Hannah. You and I—we are done. We've been done for a long time. You're not getting in between me and my family." He wheeled around and hurried after his pregnant girlfriend, calling her name.

Sara slipped an arm around Hannah's shoulder. "Come on. Come on, let's walk just over there and sit."

"Breathe, Hannah." Beth sounded worried. "Seriously, breathe. You'll get through this. I promise."

CHAPTER 12

"At least he didn't empty your account." Beth blew out a breath of relief.

"He left about half the money." Hannah punched in a small amount and took the cash from the ATM. She felt numb. Like her body didn't belong to her. Stupidly, she looked at the wad of bills in her hand before she tucked them into her purse. "It's enough to get me through a couple of months." If Alex let her stay rent-free in his bookstore apartment. Maybe she could pay him back later.

"Let's go have lunch," Sara said resolutely. "You always need something yummy in your belly when dealing with men. I'm thinking...quiche, with lots of bacon bits and egg. And a glass of cool white wine."

"I don't think I can eat," Hannah murmured. All morning, she'd felt like throwing up. Her stomach was better now, but bacon and egg quiche sounded too rich.

"Then you stick to the white wine." Sara hooked her arm under Hannah's.

"No, no. You need to eat something, darling. The sooner, the better. You also *definitely* need a lawyer." Beth took Hannah's other arm. "I'm sure Sara can help."

"You have my card," Sara said and patted the pocket where she carried her work phone. "Let me talk to my boss before you set up a meeting. He's pricey, but I'll talk him down."

Hannah managed a small smile. "Thank you. Without you two, I'd be curled in the fetal position on the ground at the farmers market."

"Women have to stick together. We're like book club sisters, even if our first meeting is still on the horizon," Sara said, guiding them toward the bustling heart of the small town, where quaint restaurants and cozy cafés lined the sun-kissed streets. "I'm not sure if you've fully realized yet just how unfairly your husband is treating you."

"I see it," Hannah said. "I just can't believe it. He's led two lives. One with me, and one with...with..."

"Honestly? I don't think she knew about you either," Beth said. "And hallelujah with that situation. She's pregnant with his child. He probably told her he'd finally got that house he'd promised her all these years."

"Don't." Hannah gently disentangled herself from her book club sisters, her mind still reeling from those words. "I can't focus on the house right now. I've been wanting to get it back for so many years."

Humming a sympathetic sound, Beth stopped in front of an unassuming eatery. A blue-and-silver sign announced its name to be *Le Pélican*. "What do you feel worse about, Hannah? Losing that man or your mother's house?"

Hannah shook her head. Right before the disastrous run-in on the farmers market, she'd have answered differently. It shattered her heart, the fragments piercing through her layers of denial and optimism. The rupture was irreversible. The break was done.

She inhaled, forcing herself to let the old dream go. What was left? "Losing the house. Evan is a stranger to me. I don't know who he is anymore." The words surprised Hannah. But they were true; she could feel it in the tingling in her fingertips and the lifting of her spine. She squared her shoulders. "That's right. Who is he? Not my husband. I refuse to feel bad about losing him anymore." But the moment the words left her lips, she crumbled into tears.

"There, there. You're right, but your head is ahead of your heart," Sara said soothingly.

"No!" Hannah wiped her palm over her face. "No. It's my heart that's ahead of my head. It hurts. Bad. Um." Sniffling, she looked for a menu. "Do they serve wine here?"

"They very much do. Let's get you fixed up with a glass and some of the best food this town has to offer." Beth pulled open the door, and they stepped into the tiny restaurant.

It smelled delicious, the fragrance warm and comforting like a mother's hug. There were only five tables, but they were beautifully laid with immaculate, snowy tablecloths, gleaming silverware, and sparkling crystal.

"Bonjour, Beth. Sara." A matronly woman, dressed in a knee-length blue dress with a Peter Pan collar, appeared from the back. "Any table you want. I'll bring you...tea? Lemonade?" She squinted appraisingly.

Beth gestured toward the table closest to the window, and they sat. "Do you still have that Chardonnay I tried last time I was here?"

Without missing a beat, the woman nodded. "And who is this?"

"This is Hannah Banner," Sara said and sat, hanging her purse over the back of her chair. "She used to live here. Hannah, meet Mama Marta, also known as Marta Beaufort. She's from Brittany in France, and she's the best cook in the world."

"Hi." Hannah tried to smile.

"Her dirtbag husband got another woman pregnant and locked Hannah out of her mother's house," Beth whispered loudly, causing Hannah to drop into her chair, put her elbows on the snowy cloth, and hide her face in her hands.

"Ah," Marta Beaufort said. "Ma poor chérie. I remember your mother. If ever there was a Tiffany alive, she is it."

"Oh." Hannah wasn't sure what that meant.

"You don't want the Chardonnay. You need the Pinot Grigio." Marta smiled comfortably. "It is a special year, and I don't give it to just anybody. You'll see." She waved her hand. "I'll be back soon."

Hannah dropped her hands and leaned back in the comfortable chair. "I feel a bit better. Why, I'm not sure."

"No woman, dead or alive, can resist Marta's cooking," Sara promised. "She's a bit tyrannical about what you can and cannot order, but she's rarely wrong."

"I love it." Beth shifted, making herself comfortable. "It effectively relieves you from having to make any decisions yourself. It's all mental labor, you know. I read that we only have a certain amount of decisions we can make in a day before it becomes stressful." She tapped a thoughtful finger on her knee. "Maybe that's why the food is so expensive?"

"Expensive?" Nervously, Hannah smoothed the fine tablecloth. "Maybe I shouldn't order food, you guys. I don't know what will happen when I run out of funds. I don't have a job yet, and there's no library in town."

"Lunch is on me, ladies," Beth announced firmly. "Don't even worry about it."

"Thank you!" Sara smiled brightly. "Excellent. I have to admit that I don't come here as often as I'd like because of the prices. Oh, darn." Her work phone rang, and with an apologetic look, she grabbed it and walked outside to answer it.

A moment later, Marta returned, carrying a silver tray with a bottle of Pinot Grigio and a basket full of small, warm, toasty-golden puff pastries that she set on the table. "I just made these. They are called *gougères*; say it like *goo-zher*." She poured the wine. "Try. Try. It will make you feel better."

"What are they?" Beth took one and studied it, turning it in her fingers.

Hannah followed her example. A moment ago, she didn't think she could eat. Now, her stomach was starting to grumble.

"They're delicious, that's what they are." Marta sounded mildly annoyed. "I just told you." She set down the bottle and looked sternly at Beth. "Don't you trust me? Do you think, oh, she's only run the best restaurant in town for the last thirty years, but she doesn't know how to cook?"

Beth sat up, blinking rapidly. "Oh, no. I don't think that at all, Marta."

Hannah smiled and bit into her appetizer. It was, it turned out, a light and airy cheese puff made with gruyère cheese, baked golden brown, and served warm. "So good!" she said, catching a crumb with her hand.

Marta nodded accusingly. "Yes. There. So good."

Beth smiled. "Of course it's good, Marta. Everything you make is good."

"It's the best," Marta insisted.

"They *are* the best." Hannah reached for another. "Try it, Beth."

Beth did, closing her eyes and clearly savoring the creamy, light flavor and irresistible consistency.

"Aha!" Triumphantly, Marta whisked her tray off the table and clamped it under her arm. "I will be back!"

CHAPTER 13

S orry about that, ladies." Sara came back inside, tucking her phone away and dropping on her chair. "I wouldn't miss this little lunch break for the world, but I'll have to work later tonight. The firm needs my superpowers." She sighed. "It's nice to be needed—but I wish my husband would find a job already. I haven't taken a vacation since the pandemic started."

"Oof." Beth gave her a pitying look. "I didn't know he lost his job. I'm sorry, Sara."

"It's all right. Lots of people are in my shoes, aren't they? Anyways—I see the wine has arrived!" Sara took the narrow stem of her crystal glass. "Cheers. Here's to good men and seaside houses and sudden riches."

"To us," Beth added.

"To the book club." It was all Hannah could think of. Neither good men, seaside houses, or sudden riches were in her future. In fact, the opposite was staring her in the face. She lifted her glass, and they all drank deeply from the cool, crystal gold. It had light, floral aromas and a crisp acidity that quickly chased away the bad taste thinking about her future had put in Hannah's mouth. She took another sip, long and thirsty. "This is good."

"This here is good too." Marta was back with a larger tray. "You get my truffle risotto, ma chérie. Truffle oil cures the belly and the heart." She put a large plate of fragrant creamy rice finished with a generous shaving of Parmigiano-Reggiano in front of Hannah.

Sara got a big bowl of velvety white soup, served with a warm, crusty baguette. "For you, it is lobster bisque, rich with cream and lobster meat." Moving surprisingly quick, Marta dipped back into the kitchen to get the last plate. Piled high on it was pasta in a rich Parmesan cream sauce and topped with juicy grilled shrimp and fresh herbs. "Beth, ma petite, eat fettuccine. It will put some...how do you say? Meat. Meat on your bones. It will plump you up nicely and make you look happy."

"I will," Beth said meekly. "Thank you kindly, Marta."

Satisfied, Marta put a hand on her hip, surveying the table. "Oui. It is good," she said to herself, clearly content with her work. "Bon appétit, ladies." Without waiting for a response, she left.

Hannah dipped her sparklingly clean spoon into the truffle risotto, the enticing aroma wafting up to tease her taste buds. It was a symphony of deep flavors: creamy Arborio rice blended perfectly with earthy mushrooms, luxurious truffle oil, and a touch of fresh thyme. Parmesan shavings cascaded over the hot rice, melting into a savory embrace, while an aromatic drizzle of truffle oil completed the masterpiece. The result was a silky, creamy delight, and the most comforting food Hannah could remember ever eating—with possibly the exception of her mother's Sunday morning pancakes.

For the next few minutes, all they could do was eat and drink. Like a magic potion, the meal demanded all of Hannah's attention. Bite after bite and sip after sip, food and drink brought Hannah back into her body. The last lingering numbness from the shock slowly left as her stomach filled.

When Sara finally paused between spoonfuls of lobster and said, "I swear this bisque was made by aliens. Humankind doesn't have this kind of technology," Hannah was able to chuckle at the joke. Almost, she felt like herself again.

As if they'd silently agreed on lighter, more pleasant topics, they started chatting about the book they were supposed to be reading for the club. Beth had downloaded the e-book and had started in on the first few pages, while Sara was already several chapters in.

"So the detective doesn't want to take on the case?" Hannah made sure. "Why not? Isn't she good?"

"She's good, but she took the job back home so she could slow down. She's got other things to do," Beth explained. "Like, her mother's getting on in years. She needs her daughter to come home."

Sara weaved her head and refilled their glasses. "It's not clear what's going on with the detective's mother. I'm not sure she even likes her daughter."

"That's not it," Beth said quickly. "The mother never got over the disappearance of the detective's sister. I can't imagine what she's going through, losing a child."

At the mention of children, and mothers, Hannah suddenly remembered again why she was in the little restaurant. She put down her fork and wiped her mouth. The wine bottle was empty, but she drained her glass and tried to get the last drop out. With a sigh of defeat, she set the bottle down again. "I can't have children," she said quietly. "Not even with the clinic's help. We tried for years before giving up."

"I'm sorry." With a look of concern, Sara put her hand on Hannah's. "That's rough. You didn't want to adopt?"

Hannah shrugged. "Evan wanted to have his own. But when it was clear it wasn't going to happen for us..." She frowned at the memory of that difficult time. "I thought we eventually came out the other end being okay. Clearly, I was wrong."

She didn't mention the tears, the hope every month before her period, the crushing disappointment when it arrived despite their efforts, or the look on Evan's face each time she had to deliver the bad news. For years, their intimate life had revolved around her cycle, until both of them found it more of a burden than a joy. The spark they once shared never rekindled.

"It's *not* your fault, do you hear?" Beth said quietly. "He's a grown man; if he's not happy and wants to leave the relationship, he should have the decency to tell you. He's got no business having a girlfriend while he's still married to you." She huffed in frustration. "Let alone getting her pregnant."

Hannah swallowed hard, her thoughts swirling with doubt. "Do you think he still loves me? I mean, after so many years...how can there be nothing left?"

Her new friends looked at her with a mixture of helplessness, compassion, and confusion on their faces.

She slumped back in her chair. "I guess not."

"I don't know if your husband even knows what love *is*," Sara said softly. "He's hung you out to dry, sweetheart."

"I come with le dessert!" The door to the kitchen swung open dramatically, and Marta reappeared with another full tray. This time, three tall glasses teetered on it.

"What do we get?" Sara asked happily.

"Peach melba parfaits. I haven't remembered them in months, but it felt good to make them now." Marta stacked their empty plates and bowl and carried them off, humming a tune. Hannah was glad to see that preparing *le dessert* had restored her good mood.

Hannah plunged the long silver spoon that had arrived with the peach melba into her parfait. Luscious layers of ripe peaches, raspberry sauce, and vanilla bean whipped cream were garnished with toasted hazelnut bits. Lost in thoughts of Evan, Allison, and the unsettling scene at the marketplace, she mechanically consumed her dessert while Beth and Sara discussed the book.

"You should get the paperback at the bookstore."
Sara shook her head at Beth.

"But I like the e-book." Beth looked confused. "It's
so convenient! And you can download it right away.
Plus, you don't have to carry the book with you. I love
paperbacks, but I don't take them with me. They just
get dog-eared. On the other hand, I always have my
phone."

"Uh-oh." Smiling despite her misery, Hannah licked
her spoon clean. As a librarian, she'd heard this dis-
cussion many times.

"I agree." Sara leaned forward. "But, Beth, it's hard
for small bookstores right now. I'm sure Alex is struggling to keep the doors open, and I really don't want
the bookstore to go out of business again. He needs
that store." She sank back again. "*I* need it. Everyone
should buy their books there. You too."

Hannah's eyebrows rose in alarm. She'd had no idea
the store was on the brink. Of course it was. Not
many people supported tiny independent bookstores
in the times of online subscriptions, e-books, and
lightning-fast downloads. "We need to do something,"
she said. "He's so kind and helpful—we should help
him."

Beth looked at her, incredulous. "I agree. But you
have enough on your plate, don't you?"

Hannah nodded. "I need to talk with Evan when he's
calmed down. I need to know what's really going on."

"You already know what's going on," Sara interjected,
a note of impatience in her tone. "You know exactly

what's going on, Hannah! What you need is a good *lawyer*."

Mute, Hannah nodded. Of course Sara was right. Obviously, her marriage was over; there was no denying it. But she still needed time to process the depth of Evan's betrayal. Just like a good diet couldn't shed years of accumulated weight in a week, Hannah couldn't simply let go of her attachment in one fell swoop. Facing the truth all at once was too daunting. She needed to navigate the pain step by step, one little admission at a time.

"Et voilà." The door flapped open and closed once more as Marta brought out the check and whisked the glasses away. "No more wine and food for you, my dears. I have to close now. My son called and asked me to watch the grandchildren. Much as I adore them, they must not enter *Le Pélican* with their grubby little hands. So I have to go to his house."

Sara glanced at the bill, and her eyes widened. "Are you sure? It's a lot."

"Ah! Good food is not cheap! And the wine was special, to make better the mood." Marta looked unrepentant.

"It was worth every penny, and of course I'm sure, Sara. Don't you dare chip in, I already called dibs." Beth whisked the bill over and pulled out her wallet, counting notes onto Marta's silver tray.

Content, Marta planted a kiss on each available cheek, and then she shooed their little flock out of the door, locking the door behind them and flipping the handwritten sign from *open* to *closed*.

Hannah was not happy. But she was full, and warm, and much better than when she'd stumbled into *Le Pélican*. "Let's meet tomorrow night," she said, a plan forming in her head as they said their goodbyes. "Let's meet at the bookstore, books in hand, and have our first proper book club meeting."

Sara nodded. "I'll just have to clear the time with Andy and the kids. Talking about which, I really should get back to work." She turned to leave, walking backward and waving. "Bye, ladies! Thanks for lunch! I'm looking forward to seeing you tomorrow. Read all the way to chapter five!"

"Will do! Bye-bye." Hannah waved back, sorry to see Sara go.

"I'll see you tomorrow." Beth hugged her. "Hang in there tonight, Hannah. I'll bring cheese and wine and crackers."

CHAPTER 14

"Y ou slept in my pajamas again." Alex, morning-rough and disheveled, blinked at Hannah from the bottom of the staircase.

"Sorry. You said it was okay." Hannah tugged on the shirt, making sure she was adequately covered in the salty breeze coming from the sea. The sun was out, and the sapphire sky was cloudless, but the air was still cool from the night.

His grin widened. "I didn't say it wasn't."

She returned his smile. "You know, it's nice that you still use PJs."

"They were an accidental online order. Thought it was only pants. You can have the tops if you like them." The hint of amusement softened his rugged features as he rubbed his jaw. "Coffee?"

"Yes, please." Smiling back, Hannah pushed her messy bed-curls out of her face. The first silver strands glinted in them, reflecting the morning sun like tinsel.

When he returned with two steaming mugs, Alex was dressed in dark jeans and a faded Henley shirt, sleeves pushed back from his forearms.

"I can come down," Hannah called out, leaning on the railing. "Might be easier!" She snagged the washed undies she'd put out with her other clothes last night to dry and tossed them back into the apartment. She'd picked up an extra pack at the pharmacy the day before, together with a toothbrush and a few other necessities.

He shook his head in a way that told Hannah he'd rather eat his arm than admit his knee was in pain climbing the old stairs.

"Thanks very much." She took the mug he handed her and sat on the top step to enjoy the hot drink and the panoramic view of the brilliantly blue ocean. Already, it felt like a comforting morning ritual. "What's your injury?"

"My eye?" Slowly, he lowered himself on the step below her. "The cornea is shot. Quite literally. Well, almost. It got scraped. We were ambushed, and I hit the ground a little harder than was good for my face."

"You can't see at all from it?"

"Maybe surgery will set it straight."

"And the leg?" She warmed her hands on the mug. It had a puppy on it.

"And the leg..." He sipped his coffee. "There's nothing wrong with the leg, at least according to the doc. I don't know. It's stiff. The joint doesn't like to bend. If nothing's wrong, I'm just a bit crazy."

Hannah hesitated for a moment, then yielded and lightly touched his arm in sympathy. "It's okay to be a bit crazy," she reassured him with a smile. "Nothing wrong with that."

He glanced at the spot on his arm where she had touched him, a subtle reaction that didn't escape Hannah's notice. "Erm. Yep. Yes. I guess so."

Hannah wanted to ask about the details of his eye injury, but he hadn't offered any information, and she didn't want to pry. "So...I saw Evan yesterday," she said awkwardly. "We ran into each other at the farmers market."

"You did?" Alex took another long sip from his mug, his gaze fixed on the crystalline ocean sparkling like an immense jewel beyond the bluff.

"Yep," she said, looking down at her hands cradling the warm puppy mug. "Turns out, he's had a girlfriend all along. They've been seeing each other for four years. And...she's pregnant and ready to pop, judging from the size of her belly."

Alex pulled in a sharp breath. "For real?"

She nodded. "For real," she murmured.

"That's..." Alex struggled to find the words, his eyes flashing with anger. "Sorry, Hannah. That's beyond bad. That's unforgivable."

"Yeah." She'd had all night to wonder about the other woman. What had they done, when, where, and how had Hannah not seen it? All those work trips to San Francisco... Sometime during the long night, she'd counted them on her phone's calendar app. There had been enough trips and long weekends for Evan to split his time fifty-fifty between his wife and his girlfriend.

"I truly was so stupid," she whispered. "So stupid. I should have known."

"No." The word sounded harsh. "You trusted him. Didn't you?"

"Yes," she said. "I did."

"It never occurred to you that there was someone else, didn't it?" He lowered his head.

"No," she said and looked at the back of his neck. "It did not."

"And why should it?" He lifted his mug, but it was already empty. Alex set his empty mug on the stairs. "Don't beat yourself up for being trusting and loving and everything you should be."

Her cheeks flushing warm with the unexpected praise, Hannah handed him her own mug. "That's the nicest thing anyone has ever said to me." She smiled. "Here. I only took a sip. No cooties."

He glanced at her over his shoulder with his one eye before taking the mug from her hands and drinking deeply. "I didn't have a good night," he murmured. "Sometimes my knee makes it hard to sleep."

The expression in his eye spoke volumes, revealing more than his words ever could. "It's not only the injuries—you're still hurting from your own relationship, aren't you?" Hannah asked quietly. "Whatever happened to you—I'm sorry."

"Ah." He handed the mug back. "Nothing happened to me, Hannah. I'm fine." Gripping the railing, he pulled himself up.

"We can be miserable together," Hannah said with a smile, trying to lighten the mood after probing too deeply. If he didn't want to talk about it, she'd respect his choice.

"I'm not miserable."

"Okay," she said soothingly. The sea breeze picked up, carrying the scent of roses blooming below. Shaking her curls back, she took another sip, the mug still carrying the faint, comforting scent of Alex.

He rubbed his jaw, the rasping sound of his beard stubble filling the air, looking like he was considering something. Suddenly, he said, "When I left Afghanistan, I was looking forward to seeing my wife. I was going to surprise her, make one of those sappy videos about returning home for our future kids. I figured she'd be glad to have me back. Minus one eye but alive, you know?"

"Yes," Hannah said quietly. "Of course." She braced herself for the inevitable hard turn of his story. There was no wife tucked away in Alex's bookstore.

"Yeah, there was nobody home to surprise. She'd gone on a camping trip with a girlfriend. At first, I was surprised. She'd never agreed to go camping with me. Well, when the credit card bills arrived, I figured out pretty quick that it wasn't a camping trip. And it wasn't a girlfriend either."

"Oh, no. Alex..."

He turned to Hannah, a wry smile tugging at the corners of his lips. "Okay, so I was gone longer than I should have been, even if it wasn't by choice. It happens. I'm over it. But, seriously...I know the guy, and let's just say he's not the sharpest tool in the shed. The only thing he's ever read are scoreboards and recipes for making protein shakes. Sometimes I wonder. What did I do to make her pick him?"

"I'm so sorry," she said softly, setting her mug down and clasping her hands between her knees. "You really didn't deserve to be treated like that." She'd been lonely plenty of times when Evan was gone. She'd arranged her life without taking another lover.

"Here's the thing." Alex paused, inhaling deeply to steady himself. "When I came back, she was pregnant. Like your story, but in reverse."

"Oh." Hannah's eyes widened, her heart aching for him. "Uh..."

"Yeah, I don't know." A frown knotted his brow. "Could be mine. Could be his. Right now, it's his."

"According to...?" Hannah couldn't imagine not knowing whether she was the baby's parent. She'd have sleepless nights too.

"According to my ex."

Hannah didn't know what to say. "Did you do a test?" she finally asked.

"No. I can't..." He spread his hands in a gesture encompassing the little bookstore, his eye, his knee, the ocean, everything. "I can barely..." His hands dropped again. "Besides, what am I going to do? He should be with his mother. I—it doesn't matter. At least not to a baby."

"You *matter*." Hannah's heart swelled at the vulnerability in his voice, recognizing the unspoken fear beneath his words: I can't be a dad. And maybe Alex was right, at least for the moment. He was injured, and the store was teetering on the edge of bankruptcy, with a freeloader living on top.

"His name is Noah," Alex said, his voice catching slightly.

"I'm really sorry, Alex," Hannah said sincerely, touched by his vulnerability.

He waved the sympathy away with a dismissive gesture. "I'm fine. I'd better get back down."

"Are you all right?" She held her breath, half expecting him to turn and storm off, the way Evan did when things got too emotional.

Instead, Alex turned back to her. "Yeah. Yeah. Hey, Hannah—sorry about unloading. Those sleepless nights get me sometimes, but I'm fine." His smile looked strained. "I should go. I've got a lot to do."

She smiled back. Instead of bringing her down, his willingness to share his own messy situation had made her feel less alone. She was no longer the only person going through a messy breakup full of betrayal and hurt. She wasn't the only one who would be rebuilding her life from scratch.

"Can I help with anything? What do you have to do?" she asked. "I know books. Can I lend a hand in the store?"

"Actually, the store is closed today. That eye surgery I mentioned? It's happening today. Shouldn't take too long; maybe a couple hours or so. But I don't think I want to unpack book boxes afterward."

"The surgery is today? Are you ready for it?"

He nodded. "I figured I was one tough guy, but the thought of a scalpel cutting into my eyeball..." He blew out a breath. "That's not my thing."

"That's nobody's thing." Hannah smoothed the PJ top over her knees, trying not to paint the image in her mind. "So how can I help?"

His blue gaze landed on her, a hint of uncertainty in it. "I need a ride," he said after a while. "They won't let me drive back on my own. But it's a half-hour drive to the hospital in Mendocino Cove. I tried to get an Uber while I was making coffee, but it looks like there are no drivers in the area today."

"You got it." She smiled, glad she could for once help him. "It's the least I can do, Alex."

"Oh. All right." He ran a hand through his short hair. "You sure?"

"It's not a problem. I'm happy to help out."

He looked at her, his one eye blue and wide open. Then he abruptly turned. "I should get ready."

"When do we leave?"

"In an hour." He was already making his way down the stairs, his grip on the railing so tight for support his knuckles blanched. "Is that okay?"

"Sure." She watched him make his escape. Why was it so hard for men to ask for help? He hadn't hesitated to let her, a perfect stranger, stay in his apartment. But when it came to asking for a ride himself...

Hannah picked up the empty mugs and brought them into her tiny kitchen where she washed them out. Then she threw open all the windows, letting the rose-scented breeze and bright sunlight stream into the apartment and warm the floorboards while she fluffed her down pillow, turned back her duvet, and took a quick shower. Though her washed clothes were clean, they still felt a bit damp, but she knew they would dry quickly.

The night before, she had searched her car and, to her delight, found an old phone charger in the glove compartment. She also brought up a wide comb, a handful of bobby pins, her favorite lip gloss, and a pair of brown leather sandals she had found tucked under her seat. After dressing in her jeans and T-shirt, Hannah slipped into the sandals, raked order into her short curls, pinned them out of her face, and swiped pink gloss on her lips. She decided the light tan from sitting on the seawall suited her.

But then she remembered the image of Evan's pregnant girlfriend—how pretty, young, and bright she'd looked. She thought of the two of them around her mother's house, holding hands, kissing in the garden... Hannah cleared her throat, trying to push away the unwanted images rising in front of her mind's eye.

Four years of images.

Quickly, she grabbed a sweater from the closet and made her way downstairs with the clean mugs. "Alex?" The bookstore's back door stood wide open, and Hannah stepped inside. "Are you in here?"

"In the store," she heard his voice. "Come here, Hannah. I want to show you something."

CHAPTER 15

Hannah left the clean mugs next to the coffee maker and walked down the corridor to the store. To her left, she glimpsed another small room. In the corner stood a collapsible military field cot. The sheets were neatly done, and on the chair in the corner was a folded pile of Alex's clothes. She hurried past, a pang of curiosity tugging at her. His leg was not physically injured—but it was stiff enough that he chose not to live in the cozy apartment upstairs?

Alex sat behind the counter, a cane leaning on the wall beside his stool. In front of him laid an open notebook.

"Knock-knock," Hannah announced her presence and went to stand by him. "What do you want to show me?"

"This. I thought it was somewhere in the store, but I didn't want to say anything in case it got lost." He slid the notebook over to Hannah. "It's the meeting log of your grandmother's book club."

"Really?" Interested, Hannah leaned over the book. It was opened on the first page, and there, in a girly, loopy hand, was her grandmother's name. It was followed by two other names. She pointed. "Are they Beth and Sara's grandmothers?"

"As far as I know." Alex nodded. "The club used to meet here, Gramps told me." He smiled. "The old man had a lot of good stories about the store. I think he had a crush on at least one of your grandmothers. They were all in their twenties together, and he wasn't married yet."

Hannah smiled. "Did he say he had a crush on the book club women?"

Alex grinned and shook his head. "Never. Once he met my grandmother, he worshipped the ground she walked on. But he had a light in his eyes when he talked about the book club meetings in his store. They always asked him to pick their next book, and he enjoyed that. Apparently, they loved mysteries and adventure books."

Eyes flying over the log entries, Hannah asked, "Do you know how old they were when they had the book club? I barely remember my grandmother. She died just before I turned five years old."

Alex shrugged. "They would all have been in their early twenties."

"They read Beatrice Sterling!" Hannah was delighted to see one of her favorite authors listed on the first page of meeting notes.

"Sterling?"

Hannah looked up. "She was an enigmatic figure in the literary world of the early twentieth century. She was born into a wealthy family in New England, where she rebelled against the role society expected of her."

"As in?" A crooked smile lifted the corner of Alex's mouth.

"As in, she refused her suitor and became a writer. I wish we knew more about her, but Sterling worked to maintain a mysterious persona. She refused to join the literary circles of her times and left the newspapers and magazines guessing. We found out a bit more about her now, but not much by any means." She tipped her head, surprised he asked. "You haven't heard of her?"

The crooked smile turned into a grin. "Of course I have."

She smiled back at him. "Did you just test my knowledge of Beatrice Sterling?"

The smile reached his eye, brightening the blue even more. "Anyone can claim they're a librarian. Few can pass the test."

She chuckled and held up the logbook. "Can I have this?"

He spread his hands generously. "All yours. I suggest showing it to Beth and Sara. They were their grandmothers too."

"That's why I want to keep it. But it looks like it was my grandmother who kept the log." Hannah pointed at a statement to the effect on the first page, where the three women had charmingly declared their official functions in the club. "See? It's all right if I'm the new keeper."

"I think it'd be a fitting tribute if you continued it." Alex rose from his stool, testing his stiff leg before putting weight on it. "There's plenty of blank space left in there. I reckon your grandmas would appreciate you picking up where they left off."

"I'd like that too. We could even read Sterling next." Hannah closed the book and put it on the shelf behind the counter for safekeeping. "I love all her books."

"Any favorite?" He grabbed the cane and leaned on it as he walked toward the door.

"Yes!" Hannah followed him, grabbing the bag he'd obviously packed for the hospital stay and forgotten by the chair. "*Whispers of the Moon*! It's Sterling's debut novel. There's nothing like a secluded mansion in the English countryside and a tale of love, betrayal, and the supernatural. Don't you think so?"

"Well, I'm more of a thriller kind of guy," he said dryly. "But *Whispers of the Moon* had a big literary impact at the time."

"Actually, I take that back," Hannah said eagerly, happy to talk about books. "My favorite is *Echoes of Eternity*." She sped past Alex to open the door. "I love stories where strangers are brought together by fate and their lives interconnect. Plus, it's set in the bustling streets of Paris during the Roaring Twenties. Ah! The movie was great too, but the original was so much better than the remake." She sighed as the images of heroines struggling with destiny, redemption, and the enduring power of love came back to her.

"Not a thing wrong with my hands. I can open doors just fine." Alex followed her outside.

"But then again, *Secrets of the Sea* is also a big favorite of mine," Hannah continued. "Like, a *big* favorite."

"If you step aside, I can lock the door," Alex said patiently.

"Did you read it? *Secrets of the Sea* was her last. So heartbreaking!"

"No. I have not." He pulled out an old-fashioned bearded key.

"It's set on the windswept shores of a remote island off the coast of Maine. There's mystery and romance and adventure, and a young woman's journey of self-discovery as she uncovers the hidden secrets of her family's past."

"I wish I could uncover the secret of *my* past," Alex murmured. "Like, what did Gramps do with his bootleg liquor? Every now and then, I lay awake at night, wondering where it all went."

Smiling, Hannah opened the passenger door of her car for him. "Maybe he drank it. Here, I'll take the cane."

"Maybe he did, and it's not a cane, it's a stick I like to carry around to look more distinguished. But thanks." Alex handed her the cane and folded his six-foot-something frame into the car. "In fact, I know he drank it."

"I thought you lay awake, wondering about it?" Hannah teased him as she stowed the cane in the trunk and got in the car herself.

Alex closed his eye and leaned his head back. "I do a lot of things at night," he said, clearly trying to sound dignified.

"I bet you do." Hannah strapped in and pulled out her phone. "Okay. Where are we going?"

"I'll send you the address. What's your phone number?"

Hannah gave Alex her phone number, he sent her the address to the hospital in Mendocino Cove, and a few moments later, they were on their way.

"That's my mother's place there," she said quietly when they drove over the bluff and pointed it out. "Now Evan lives there."

"It's a great house." Alex rolled down his window for a better look as they passed. "I'd much rather think of *you* living there. He can't just claim it for himself. That's not how this works."

"I'm starting to think you're right," she murmured. "But I still..." She broke off, a warm flush of shame coloring her cheeks as her mind flicked to all the things Evan had done to her.

"Don't tell me you still love him!" Alex's voice dropped to a growl. "You deserve better."

She moistened her lips. "You know, at the farmers market yesterday?"

"When you met his pregnant girlfriend? Yes. What about it?" He rolled his window back up, a frown shadowing his face as he turned to her. "Did he bother you?"

Hannah flicked the blinker to turn as she turned into Mendocino Cove. "I wasn't the only one who was shocked. She didn't realize I existed either. Evan never told her that he was married and had a wife. She thought he was buying their little family a house at the coast so they could finally live together."

Alex rubbed his hands over his face. "Shoot." He dropped them in his lap and looked at her. "Hannah, I apologize on behalf of all the male dirtbags you have and will encounter."

She glanced back at him. The eye patch made it hard to read him at the best of times, but he looked as sincere as he sounded. "It's not your fault. No more than it is my fault that your ex went camping."

Alex crossed his arms. "If you want me to tell Evan to get out of your house, I will. No problem. In fact, I'd enjoy it."

"Oh!" She almost laughed as she pulled on the redwood-lined road to the hospital. "Are you offering to beat up my unfaithful husband?"

"Call it what you like."

She glanced at him, hoping he wasn't being serious. "Well, thank you, I suppose. Unfortunately, challenging Evan to fisticuffs in a back alley isn't going to solve anything."

"I don't know," Alex said thoughtfully and scratched the stubble on his chin. "I think it might."

CHAPTER 16

S ara picked up the phone and pressed the key to call her husband.

"Sara? What's up?" Andy sounded sleepy.

"Hi, honey." Sara's right eye was dry from staring at her computer screen all day, and she rubbed it. "Um, I'm going to go to my book club meeting tonight. I just wanted to let you know that I won't be home to make dinner."

Her husband's frown was almost audible. "What book club?"

"A couple of friends and I come together to read and discuss books." She sounded too formal and took a breath to relax. It wasn't a crime to belong to a book club. Not even when you had a husband who was perpetually frustrated with his lot in life and two teenagers who, according to themselves, couldn't figure out how to boil pasta.

"I'm sorry," Andy said pointedly. "But my parents are coming over for dinner tonight, Sara."

"Oh, right." Someone's parents were always coming over for dinner. At least they weren't hers.

"Yeah, *oh right*," he mocked her.

Sara drew in a breath. Andy really knew how to push her buttons. "Honey, you'll just have to do without me."

"What do you mean?"

She raised an eyebrow, annoyed. "Just cook something and eat without me."

"What do you mean, cook something? Like what? You're the cook in the house. Don't just dump your responsibilities on me. It's disrespectful to me. Just because I was laid off doesn't mean—"

Sara's grip on the phone tightened. "Andy," she interrupted his tirade. "You're a grown man who's eaten thousands of dinners. Just make something. It doesn't have to be fancy. Your dad wants to watch the soccer game with you. There's beer and chips for snacking."

"What about my mother?"

Sara knew he was stalling, trying to guilt her into coming home because he didn't want to be the only one entertaining his parents. "She'll watch the game too," she said patiently. "Honey, come on. I just want to see my friends and talk about books for a while."

"Either you lock yourself into your room to draw, or you meet with your friends," he complained, changing tactics.

Sara's forehead crumpled. "I'm absolutely *not* either locked in my room or meeting with friends," she said, her voice cooling. "What are you talking about? If I'm not working, I'm at home, cooking and cleaning or driving kids around. I can't even remember the last time I had a moment to draw or meet with friends. We literally just reconnected. I'd like to see them for one night, to talk about books."

Andy inhaled loudly. "Well, I guess you already made your choice."

"I can't believe you're trying to make me feel guilty for wanting to spend a couple of hours with my friends." It was so unfair—Sara rarely ever spent an evening away from the family. "I haven't met up with friends in years. I want to enjoy it. Let me enjoy it."

"I haven't said a thing." He was defensive now. "It'd be nice if you respected my time a bit more than you do. You should have told me this morning, not spring things on me at the last minute like this."

"I forgot." Sara put her forehead into her hand. It was a lie. She hadn't forgotten at all. She simply had assumed it wouldn't be a problem. In fact, she had expected Andy would be happy for her. "I'm sorry. I forgot."

There was a pause before he replied, "So what am I going to cook?"

Andy was at home most of the day, writing job applications and playing computer games. Surely, he could come up with a meal for his parents? But now Sara felt guilty for skipping out, and worse for not telling him earlier. "I don't know," she conceded. "Maybe just order pizza."

"Order pizza," he grumbled. "Do you know how much that costs these days? My parents eat at least one between them, and the kids have one each. I'll need a bite too. That's four pizzas already, with no leftovers for the kids' school lunches tomorrow."

Or Sara... She was missing in Andy's calculation too. She bit her lip. "If you don't want pizza, you can make a big pot of spaghetti Bolognese," she suggested. "I just bought tomatoes and ground beef. Your mom loves spaghetti Bolognese."

"Maybe." He sighed. "How do I make it?"

Sara closed her eyes. They said people didn't change. But Andy *had* changed when he was laid off. Instead of standing on his own two feet and taking charge of his life, he behaved like a sulking, moping kid. Worse, he projected on Sara the authority he resented.

"How do I make it?" he repeated.

"There are plenty of recipes on the internet," she said. "Oops, I have another call. Have fun tonight. Don't wait up for me, Andy. Bye!"

"Wait! How long is your meeting going to be? And what about the kids? Do I have to do anything?"

Instead of answering, Sara hung up. Talking to Andy used to energize her. Now, it left her empty and exhausted. She didn't mind working and doing housework. She didn't mind driving the kids around until late and getting up early for work. But she wasn't her husband's babysitter. Or at least she didn't want to be.

Something had to change.

But what?

Andy was too vulnerable for sweeping discussions of deep-seated relationship issues.

"Everything okay?" Her boss, Julian Sterling, had come in and placed a file on her desk.

"Yes. Everything's good, Mr. Sterling." She nodded a little too fast, a little too long.

"You know the company couldn't do without you, don't you?" He gave her an earnest look.

"That's very kind of you to say." Her smile felt strained. At the moment, she'd like one thing that *could* do without her. But she needed the job, and she needed it badly.

"Hmm." He straightened his back, regarding her thoughtfully. Not much, Sara knew, escaped the notice of Julian Sterling. "Well, could you file the documents and prepare a summary of key points for the upcoming meeting with Mr. Brady, please?"

"Of course. Um—would it be okay if I leave after I send you the summary?"

"Yes. Yes, it is." He turned, his mind clearly busy with the next case.

Sara tucked the file where it belonged as she watched her boss walk into his office from under her eyelashes. She'd already prepared the summary and scheduled the email to get to him an hour before the meeting—therefore, she was free to leave. As soon as his door closed, she grabbed her cardigan and purse and hightailed it out of the office.

The clean sea air outside was a blessing. Sara drank it in thirstily. Leaving the car, she hurried through the streets toward the bookstore. A few steps away from it, she slowed. It was almost time for the book club to meet...but the store looked closed. The evening sunlight reflected off the dark windows, but there was no light shining inside. Something was wrong.

When she got to the door, she pulled the knob. As she'd feared, the door didn't open. She cupped her hand to the glass and peered inside. The aisles between the shelves were empty, the counter deserted.

Alex wasn't in. And neither was the book club.

With a sinking heart, Sara patted her pockets for her cell phone. All day, she'd been using the landline. She should have checked her own cell phone before coming here. "Dang!" she whispered when she glanced at the screen. There it was, the text. Hannah was with Alex at the hospital in Mendocino Cove. Their stay turned out longer than expected, so she had canceled the book club meeting. Beth had replied hours ago.

Hoping that everyone was okay, Sara also sent a quick text. Then she pushed the phone back into her pocket and wrapped her arms around herself.

It was her own fault for forgetting to check her cell. She had just been so sure that the book club would meet. She had so looked forward to it.

Feeling the cold sting of disappointment, she started walking toward the harbor, where the restaurants were. She couldn't face going home to Andy and his angry cooking. In passing, she longingly eyed *Le Pélican*. Marta's cooking would cheer her up. But the tiny restaurant was closed, and even if it had been open, it was too much of an expensive splurge.

Sara wandered on, studying posted menus in passing. But everything seemed either too expensive, or it didn't hit the spot, or she found something else to keep her from going in.

Finally, she gave up. It wasn't the restaurants, or the food, or even the prizes. The reason nothing sounded good was that she didn't want to be alone. No dinner would fix that. She had to go home after all. After all, they needed her there. Andy really didn't know how to make a good marinara. With a sigh, she turned on her heel to go to her car.

"Oh! Pardon. Excuse me."

Sara had been so lost in thought that she'd not watched where she was going. She took a step back, pressing her hand to her heart as she looked up. "Mr. Sterling! I'm so sorry. I almost ran over you."

Her boss looked surprised when he saw her face. "Sara? I thought you were still in the office!"

"I scheduled the summary to get to you when you need it and left, just as we said." Sara bit her lip.

"I didn't... Anyway, no harm done, Sara, I'm still in one piece and so are you. Were you about to go in?" Julian Sterling nodded at the door beside them.

"Uh." She hadn't even noticed that there was a restaurant there.

"Well—yes?" He smiled at her. "I've just had some good news about the Snyder case. It's all wrapped up and topped with a bow. It's done, and we won."

"Really? Congratulations!" The case had dragged on for years, and a lot had hung in the balance.

"Thank you, and right back at you; you've worked very hard to sort out the mess old Snyder left his heirs. Allow me to invite you to dinner. Consider it a well-deserved celebration."

"Oh. Um. Thank you. That's very nice of you." She smiled at him. Her boss could be absent-minded and even cold, but she'd been with him long enough to know that he was a brilliant lawyer and kind at heart. But she'd never had as much as a cup of coffee with him. It'd be awkward sitting through an entire dinner together.

She pointed a thumb over her shoulder. "I really should get home. Andy and the kids are waiting for me. I was just taking a quick walk to clear my head."

He nodded. "Good night then, Sara. I'm looking forward to that summary."

"Thanks, Mr. Sterling," she murmured. "Good night." She hitched her purse strap higher and hurried back to her car to drive home and cook her in-laws dinner.

CHAPTER 17

B eth buttoned her jacket. Standing in front of her
husband's grave, she'd lost herself in memories.
Now, despite the warm evening, her arms were bumpy
with gooseflesh and she felt cold to the core.

"I know you don't really miss my eggplant Parmesan,
dear Ben," she murmured, rubbing her arms. "I know
you're fine, wherever you are. And I also know that you
want me to be happy. I understand all of that." Slowly,
she straightened the dozen white roses she'd set on his
grave. Then she pulled a nail brush and a towel from
her bag and started scrubbing the matte black granite
of Ben's headstone.

Most beloved husband, the inscription read. She
paused to trace the words with a finger. *Forever missed,
always remembered.*

Soon, Beth was out of specks of moss and crud. She
stepped back and stowed away the cleaning supplies.
Two men with flowers—brothers who recently lost
their mom, she knew—passed by on the narrow path,
nodding at her. She returned the mute greeting; it was
her sign to leave and let others grieve their loved ones
in solitude.

She kissed her fingertips and pressed the kiss on the roses before she walked back to the tiny gravel parking lot that lay before the cemetery's cast iron gates. Back in her car, Beth checked the phone she'd left in the glove compartment.

Half of her hoped that the book club would meet after all. The visit and the memories had made her sad. It'd be nice to sit in the cozy bookstore and talk about a mystery with her friends. She'd even written down some questions. And she'd bought a big tray of cheese and cold meats for snacking.

Nobody knew that Alex had scheduled surgery for the day. Beth didn't even know what kind of surgery it was. Something to do with his eye, she thought as she let her phone sink on her lap. She should have asked Alex if he was all right. Of course she should have.

Beth closed her eyes. She hadn't asked what was happening with Ben either. A flu, she'd decided, when he'd finally told her he was tired and exhausted even though he got enough sleep. She'd put him in bed and made him chicken soup, and he, grateful she didn't ask him to go see a doctor, had complied. They'd carried on like that for a while. Not too long, not months. But a couple of weeks.

Pancreatic   cancer   was   aggressive.   Who knew—maybe those two weeks of oblivious denial could have saved him? She'd never dared to ask the doctor.

Now that he was gone, the question and the guilt would weigh her down forever.

She picked up the phone again. *What's going on?* she texted Hannah. It was an innocent little text, just a few words. But her heart was hammering as the shock of Ben's diagnosis echoed in her chest.

He's all right, Hannah texted back a moment later.

Beth didn't want to be that nosy old neighbor. But this was a wall she needed to break through. Picking up her courage, she asked for more. *Is he okay? What does he have?*

Corneal transplant, all went well!

Tell him all the best from me, Beth texted back.

I did & he says no worries. Hannah sent a smiling face.

Will you be back soon? Beth asked. She wanted to see Alex, as if only her own two eyes could make sure he was okay.

Just leaving hospital. Talk in a few!

Beth sent a heart and let out a hard breath. As if she'd just run a marathon, it took a moment of staring out the window at the scrollwork of the cemetery gates before her heartbeat slowed back to normal.

All went well. Alex was going to come back home.

She'd never heard of corneal transplants. The cornea was the translucent tissue over the eye that let light pass inside the eye, she knew. Alex's cornea must have gotten damaged in that terrible attack where he'd lost his three best friends, and now the damaged tissue had been replaced.

Did that mean he'd be able to see again with both eyes?

She'd bring Alex flowers, Beth decided as she started the car. From now on, she'd always ask if he needed anything. Alex offered his little bookstore to anyone who needed a cozy chair, a book, and a break, whether or not they ended up buying a copy. He deserved to have people look after him as well.

As Beth pulled out of the small gravel lot, she still didn't know where to go. The florist! She could make Alex a bouquet from her garden, but this time, she wanted the florist. Because if she went straight home from the cemetery, the temptation to break down would be too big.

So instead of taking the road home at the next junction, Beth turned toward Mendocino Beach. She'd go grab a bite to eat, and then she'd buy Alex some flowers and walk them over to the bookstore. Maybe Hannah needed a hand or just some company. Caring for someone—the long hours in the hospital waiting rooms, the long drives trying to soothe and encourage the patient—was taxing. Beth knew that only too well.

She parked near the beach and strolled barefoot along the water, then climbed up the warm sand and over the seawall to get to the town's tiny florist, where she asked Lisa, the young woman who ran it, to make a bouquet.

Beth was drawn to sunflowers, or the pretty pink roses and lavender, but Lisa hesitated. "This is for the owner of the bookstore?" she asked. "Wasn't he in the military?"

"Yes," Beth said. "Why?"

"He might enjoy a more manly bouquet." Lisa smiled an apology as she walked past the sunflower and rose pots deeper into the sweet-smelling store. "How about a cluster of deep red and burgundy dahlias in the middle? We could add a few orange and yellow marigolds around them and also add some aromatic eucalyptus leaves. I like the fresh scent, especially for a man who is just back from the hospital." Lisa thought for a moment. "And a few sprigs of robust greenery, like those ferns and salal leaves." She pointed them out. "They add texture and depth."

"Sure. That all sounds good." Beth watched as Lisa's skilled hands cut the flowers and sprigs she selected, arranging them in a beautiful bouquet.

When she wrapped it in green silk paper, Lisa looked up. "Anything else?" She smiled and gently laid the flowers next to the register.

"You know what? Yes." Beth cleared her throat. "I believe I'll have that bouquet of sunflowers, pink roses, and lavender after all."

"Sure." Lisa readily came out from behind the counter to collect the flowers. "Can I ask who this one's for?"

"This one's for me," Beth said and put her credit card on the counter.

"You've never bought pink roses before." Lisa raised her eyebrows in approval. "Do you want me to add some of the white roses you usually buy?"

"No." Beth smiled at her. "Those were my husband's favorites. I personally like pink better."

"Yes, of course." Lisa nodded. "Good for you, Beth. I was wondering when you'd get yourself a cheerful bouquet."

"I don't know why I didn't do it before." The heaviness that always followed Beth home from the cemetery lifted a little. Maybe flowers were the balm that helped heal her wound.

"Oh, it's simple." Lisa's young eyes had a wise look in them. "It wasn't the right time for your own flowers yet. But now it is. Now it is, and I'm glad. Everyone should get themselves flowers." She set the new bouquet on the counter and pulled out a sheet of yellow silk paper to wrap around it. Then she looked up with a smile. "Your bouquet is on the house, Beth." Smiling, she dried her hands on her red linen apron.

"Oh. Thank you, my dear." Beth shook her hand and pushed the card over to the florist. "I'm not rich, but Ben left this old woman well-provided. You're just starting out in life. I insist on paying."

"Nope." Lisa ran the card for the man-bouquet only. "That would bring me back luck. I never charge a woman for that first bouquet she buys herself. You can pay for the next one." She winked and handed Beth a pen to sign the receipt for Alex's flowers.

Beth smiled back but shook her head as she scribbled her signature. "How can you afford to do that?"

"Two reasons. One good, one not so good." Lisa tucked the slip in her drawer and closed it. "The good news: once you start, it feels so good you'll come back to buy more."

Beth felt her smile deepen. "Smart. What's the not-so-good reason?"

Lisa dipped the stems of the bouquets into plastic tubes filled with water and sealed them, handing them to Beth. "It doesn't happen nearly often enough. Definitely not so often that I'd go bankrupt."

Beth nodded. "I hear you." She took her flowers and cradled them in her arms, making sure the pretty blooms were safe and protected.

Lisa walked Beth to the open door and shaded her eyes against the last rays of the sinking sun glittering on the ocean in streaks of fire and gold. "It took *you* long enough," she said quietly, her smile mysterious as if she'd really waited for Beth to finally ask for her own flowers.

Beth nodded, acknowledging the truth, and stepped out on the street. "I'll be back soon," she promised. Then she waved and started walking toward the harbor with its restaurants.

That frutti di mare pizza tasted delicious. Maybe she'd stop by the little pizzeria and try the gnocchi and pesto? Or maybe a different pizza. And a glass of red wine. Just a small one. She'd walk it off on her way to the bookstore before getting back into her car.

Smiling, her arms full of fragrant flowers, Beth opened the door to the little pizzeria. The aroma of soft dough and sun-dried tomatoes, roasted garlic and melted Parmesan greeted her like an old friend when she stepped inside.

CHAPTER 18

As the sun dipped below the horizon and cast the world in hues of orange and pink, Hannah gently opened the passenger door for Alex. His head rested against the back, the black eye patch shielding his injured eye. With his good eye closed, he seemed peacefully asleep.

"Alex?" she murmured, lightly touching his arm. It felt firm like steel, the muscles beneath betraying their immense strength that was now so evident to her.

Of course, he had been under anesthesia during the procedure. Otherwise, he wouldn't have pulled her to him when he woke up, holding her tightly before she'd aided him from the stretcher to the wheelchair.

During the drive home, Hannah had ample time to contemplate the sensation of being enveloped by such powerful arms. Even though it had only been for a brief moment, it was confusing. Almost unsettlingly intimate. And yet, undeniably pleasant. Pleasant enough to make her heart drum with a guilty feeling of infidelity...

"Alex?" she whispered again, wiping the thought from her mind. The man had been drugged.

His eye blinked open, meeting hers. "Hi."

"Hi. We're home. Let's get you into your bed. Here, take my hand." Without waiting, Hannah took his hand. It was warm and relaxed, even though his grip was still firm. She smiled. He was still a little loopy from the meds.

"I'll tell you what, Hannah," he mumbled as she helped him out of the car. "I'd rather get shrapnel in my gut than go through eye surgery."

She took his arm, and step by step, they made their way to the door of the bookstore. "The doctors said it wasn't painful," she teased him. "And you were asleep the entire time."

"That's what I'm saying," he muttered. "I don't mind pain. I've taken plenty of pain. What I can't stand is the thought of a knife near my eyeball."

"They only took a bit of the top layer off. Just the cornea."

"And then they stitched a new one on my eye." Alex sounded nauseated.

Hannah understood. It was a wonder what doctors could do, but the details of the procedure made her queasy too. "I know. But they said everything went very well."

"I think I'm going to be sick," he murmured. "Stand back, Hannah."

"Hold out just a moment. We're almost inside." Hannah squeezed his hand. "Don't think about the surgery. Think about how you'll be able to see again! Isn't that great? Do you have the key? Shoot—Alex, the door's locked. Where's the key?"

With a groan, Alex reached his free hand over her shoulder and braced himself against the door.

Hannah was caught between him and the door. There was not enough space to turn. Slowly, she looked up. His blue eye looked down at her with a quizzical expression, almost as if he wondered how she got there.

"Don't be sick, please," Hannah said with a small voice.

"I'm...fine." The crooked smile—a bit weaker than usual—tugged on his lips, though beads of sweat glistened on his temple.

After clearing her throat twice, she could speak again. "Alex," she said, trying to sound reasonable. "You're going to faint. I need your key."

"You need my key." His face lowered toward hers. There was not much space to lower any further... Already, Hannah felt the warmth of his lips on her forehead.

Heart drumming in her chest, she let go of his hand and lifted her own, pressing it to the base of her throat. To calm her heart, to shield herself from what she couldn't handle... She didn't know what. Something important. Something she'd lost a long time ago.

Alex's face lowered again. His lips still did not touch her skin, but his breath caressed her cheeks, brushed down her throat, made her gasp.

"The key," she whispered.

"What key?" His voice was low and soft and dangerous to her heart.

Hannah closed her eyes, even though her head tipped back on its own volition. "The key to the bookstore."

"It's in my pocket."

"What pocket?"

"My jacket. My right, your left."

Hannah drew a breath and opened her eyes again. Holding his piercing blue gaze, she dropped her hand, slipping it into the left pocket of his sports jacket. Alex smiled, his lips inches from hers.

She smiled back. He wasn't as medicated as all that—he could tell his left from his right pocket, after all. "There's no key in your pocket, Alex." Her fingers brushed his side as she searched the lining.

This time, he didn't lower his head. Instead, he bent the arm bracing him against the wall. His lips touched her forehead with the lightest of touches. It moved against her burning skin as he whispered, "My bad. The other pocket then." He raised his head just enough to be able to look into her eyes.

"Mh-mm." Hannah slipped her other hand into the right pocket. Her fingers closed around the hard metal, and she pulled the key out. "Thank you," she whispered. She'd meant it to sound sarcastic but didn't manage the right tone. Instead, the two short words carried vulnerability.

"Not for the key, Hannah." His husky voice was laced with an underlying intensity, a subtle invitation that sent shivers down her spine.

With a fluid motion, Alex pushed off the wall, turning his blue gaze away from her and out on the ocean.

Hannah felt like a taut string, stretched to its limit, with emotions swirling within her like a turbulent sea. Her heart raced, caught between conflicting feelings. She was still married...wasn't she? Not really...but what did that mean? What, if anything, did that leave her free to do? Kiss a stranger she'd only just met?

Her fingers trembled as she clutched the key, and she had to try twice to finally fit into the lock. "Come on, Alex," she murmured. "Let's get you inside. You're still loopy from the meds." She pushed open the door.

"I'm not loopy, Hannah," He turned back to her. Suddenly, his body swayed, and he took a step backward.

Hannah grabbed his hand just in time to keep him upright. "Alex!" She managed to pull his arm—as heavy as a log—over her shoulder. "Come inside."

Again he teetered as if he were drunk, almost taking her down with him.

Someone rushed over from the corner and grabbed Alex's other arm. "Gotcha!" Beth laughed and dropped the flower bouquet in her hand to the ground to steady Alex.

"Beth!" Hannah exclaimed. "Great timing! Let's get him inside. He needs to lie down."

"Got it. Did the surgery go well?"

"Don't," Alex groaned. "I can do everything but eyes."

"Stop being a baby," Beth admonished him heartlessly. "I'm sure they did great."

"They *stitched*."

"That's a win!" Beth laughed her infectious, uplifting laugh again, and this time, Hannah joined her. Partly from relief, because it didn't mean anything after all—Alex was simply out of it, and she'd been married a little too long to know what to think when an attractive man wanted to kiss her.

Together, they guided Alex into the bookstore. He managed to walk, though balance seemed to be a problem. With their combined efforts, Hannah and Beth eased him onto his cot in the back room.

Beth stepped back, surveying the surroundings. "Is this where he lives?" she asked Hannah in a hushed tone, hands on her hips as she observed the spartan, dimly lit space.

"I believe so," Hannah replied, casting her eyes around the room. Not a single picture brightened the walls, and no window provided natural light. "I think... I think I'm hogging his apartment. This must be his fallback in case he can't manage the stairs."

"I can hear you." Alex closed his eyes and lay down, his hands on his chest. "And you're wrong, I can manage the stairs any old time. I just like it down here. Reminds me of Dad."

Hannah and Beth looked at each other, and then they smiled, took off his shoes, and covered him with the blanket. Then Hannah ran upstairs to get the plush down pillow to elevate Alex's head. The surgeon had said it would help with the healing. By the time she was back, Alex was fast asleep. Beth lifted his head while Hannah arranged the pillow.

"Okay." Hannah stepped back and sighed, and then she chuckled, and then she sighed again. "All in all, that went pretty well, don't you think?"

Beth went to the door. "Come on. Whatever they gave him got him good. Let's leave him to sleep it off."

"I'm just going to take his patch off," Hannah said. "I don't want it to shift tonight and poke his eye." Carefully, she loosened the strap and wiggled the patch off.

Underneath, Alex's closed eye looked perfectly normal. The surrounding skin was slightly swollen and red, but that was all. "I'll put it here," she whispered and carried the chair from the skinny desk by the wall to the bed. She put the eye patch on the makeshift nightstand. "It's right here beside you if you want it."

They switched off the light and closed the door, then made their way to the front of the bookstore.

"Are you tired?" Beth asked kindly as they passed the coffee room. "I know this sort of thing can be taxing."

"No." Hannah took a deep breath and blew it out again. "Strangely, I'm wide awake."

"Then we can still have that book club meeting!" Beth said and giggled at her little joke.

Hannah stepped into the storeroom and was surprised to see someone standing at the counter. At first, she thought a stray tourist had mistaken the open door for an invitation to wander inside, but then their visitor turned around. "Oh! Hey, Sara! It's you."

"I saw the light in the store." Sara looked back at Hannah, her eyes wary. "And I found these outside." She pointed to the bouquet Beth had dropped outside.

Sara had laid them on the counter. "What are you all doing here?"

"The book club meeting!" Beth laughed again, teasing her friend. "Did you forget?"

It was only a joke; like Hannah, Beth seemed relieved that Alex was back and doing well. But Hannah saw the shadow of hurt feelings fly over Sara's face when she heard the words.

Too late did Hannah understand what was happening.

"No," Sara said, her voice curt. "I didn't forget. Only you told me it wasn't going to happen. Thanks, guys. If I'm too much for you, you can just say so. You don't have to lie on my behalf." She turned on her heel and marched back to the door.

Nonplussed, Beth stared at Hannah. Hannah shook her head and hurried after Sara, who was already out on the street.

CHAPTER 19

"S ara!" Hannah called. "Stop! Where are you going?"

Sara turned around. The sky above had turned a velvety plum-red, and the breeze had picked up, tugging on her hair. "Home! To cook and clean and tell the kids to brush their teeth!"

"Sara, listen." Hannah stopped; chasing Sara didn't help anything. "We didn't have a book club meeting; Beth was only joking. I just came back from the hospital with Alex, and she happened to see us go in. She was just dropping off flowers for him." She drew in a breath. Now that night had fallen, the salty air cooled quickly. "Please, let's not turn this into a thing. Nobody is excluding anyone. You're just as much part of the club as me or Beth. Even our grandmothers stuck together."

Sara looked down, then up, and then she rubbed a hand over her face. "Oof. Sorry." She came walking back to Hannah. "I've been tired all day and talking to my husband tipped me over the edge. I'm sorry."

"No, it's okay." Hannah pulled her into a hug. She knew how Sara felt—after a long day of working for little or no money, Andy could easily bring her down with a few well-chosen words. "Let's go back and tell Beth we're okay. I think she's a bit shocked."

Sara hugged her back, and then they walked back to the bookstore together. "Sorry, Beth," she said sheepishly when they met again. "I was so looking forward to the meeting, and I really don't want to go back home and pick up everyone's slack, and...I was feeling a bit sorry for myself. I apologize."

"Oh, honey!" Beth threw her arms around Sara and kissed her loudly on each cheek. "I shouldn't have teased you—I was just joking. It wouldn't be a book club meeting without you!"

Sara smiled, looking both tired and relieved. "It's okay if there is. It's not you. I'm overworked and exhausted and ready to crack." She let herself fall into a cozy armchair. "I'm just not used to having real friends anymore. I was overthinking things."

"I'm going to put these into a vase," Hannah murmured and hurried to get a glass from the coffee room in the back. When she returned, Beth was sitting on a box of unpacked books, elbows on knees and hands propped in her face. "What about your family drives you nuts, Sara?"

"Oh—nothing. They're great. It's just...money's a little tight. Andy can't find a job. It's hard out there."

"I know. I'm sorry."

"And it's not even that he doesn't have an income; I don't mind working." Sara swallowed a watery smile. "But I seem to be doing everything else too. I'm the one who keeps track of the kids' needs, the household,

the groceries, the family laundry, everyone's health
and appointments, and even the pets. Cooking and
cleaning too, that goes without saying." She thought
for a moment. "Andy mows the lawn," she said then.

"That's a *lot*, Sara," Hannah said. "Nobody can do
all that without cracking every now and then."

"It's not even *that*." Sara closed her eyes and leaned
back. "I love the kids, and I'm glad I have food to
cook and a house to clean. I think...it's that I never
get to do what *I* want to do."

Hannah and Beth exchanged a look. Gently, Hannah asked, "What do you want to do, Sara?"

"I want to *draw*." Sara opened her eyes with surprise at her own words. "Oops! That came out of
nowhere."

"It didn't come out of nowhere," Beth said. "*Do* you
want to draw?"

"Yes." Again there was no hesitation. "When I close
my eyes, I see patterns. Swirls and vines and...beau-
tiful patterns that make me happy." She chuckled
helplessly. "I want to draw them. I want to design
wallpapers and tote bags and tiles. Is that silly?" She
shook her head. "Who wants to ditch their family
over a pattern of vines?"

"It's not silly," Hannah said. "It's perfectly under-
standable. You need a creative outlet."

"I do." Sara nodded slowly. "Before Andy lost his
job, I was dreaming of setting up my own printing
business. I love interior design. I really do want to
design wallpapers."

"Did you talk with Andy?" Beth asked. "It seems like he should know."

"He's not..." Sara lifted her hands and let them drop again. "No. I haven't. He's miserable, and I can't put more on him."

"Yes, you can," Hannah said quietly. "I sure wish my husband had told me he was unhappy in our marriage. Just tell him. It's part and parcel of being married." She sat on the wood floor, her back against the counter, hugging her knees. "Admittedly, I'm not the one to listen to when it comes to marriage advice."

"Now, wait a second, Hannah." Beth looked at her. "I don't know the details, but from the little I do know, it seems like it's your *husband* who shouldn't give out marriage advice."

"Takes two to tango." Hannah gave a weak smile. "I didn't want to see it, I guess. Looking back, I could've added up two and two and admitted that I wasn't part of his equation anymore."

"You loved your husband, Beth," Sara said. "How did you two stay in love?"

"In the beginning, we fought." Beth smiled. "All the time. But we were never mean to each other. Somehow, we managed to stay on the good side of the line, even if it was only by a hair's breadth. The older we got, the better we became at trusting the other with our issues before they turned into resentment and anger. That's it. It became easy."

"That sounds nice." A look of longing came over Sara's face.

"It's work," Beth said slowly. "It's trust earned, and trust given. It wasn't always easy. But once we found it worked for both of us, it was great and getting better all the time." She lowered her head. "I loved him so much."

For a while, they sat in silence. Hannah followed her own thoughts about Evan, the spectacular fail that was their marriage. Never again would she trust this man who had vowed to honor and respect her always.

How the pregnant Allison felt about trusting Evan, Hannah had no idea. After all, Allison had a baby on the way. Maybe she would give the father a second chance.

"I've felt sorry for myself long enough now." Sara looked up, and a small smile glinted in her eyes. "Y'all want to talk about the book?"

Hannah smiled back, and Beth laughed. "I have my copy if you have yours."

"I do." Sara pulled the book out of her purse.

"I'll get mine." Hannah got up and ran upstairs to get her copy. She also grabbed the block of cheese, crackers, and the bottle of red wine she'd bought at the supermarket and brought them back. On her trip to the coffee room to get plates and mugs, she stopped and quietly cracked the door to check on Alex.

He was lying just as she'd left him, eyes closed, breathing slow and regular.

Hannah was about to close the door again when he stirred. "Hannah?" he asked softly without opening his eyes. "Is that you?"

She tiptoed to his bed and took his hand. "Are you okay? Do you need painkillers?"

His eyes opened, but it was too dark to see the irises. "No. Hey." His fingers closed around her hand.

"What?" She leaned closer. "What is it?"

"I'm sorry," he whispered. "I'm sorry about earlier."

She smiled, and then, without thinking, she pressed a kiss of her own on his forehead. "It's okay. You were loopy from the meds."

He reached up and cradled her cheek in his hand for a moment. "I was not," he whispered. "It's not the meds; it's that I like you more than I should, Hannah Banana. Always have, always will." He dropped his hand again.

"Oh." Hannah straightened, her cheeks flushing. *Always have, always will?* "Um. Here." She tucked the blanket around him, feigning busyness. "You'd better sleep more, Alex. That's still the meds talking. How are your eyes?"

"I see you." He closed his eyes again. "No matter the eyes."

Hannah lingered for a moment, watching his breathing become slow and steady. When she was almost certain that Alex had drifted off to sleep, she quietly rose and left the room, softly shutting the door behind her.

"How is he?" Beth inquired when Hannah returned with the mugs for the wine.

"All right, I think," Hannah replied, feeling the warmth spread across her cheeks. "I can't quite tell what the meds are doing to him."

"Whatever it is that he has..." Beth smiled and sandwiched a slice of Gouda cheese between two crackers.

"I'm not sure it's only the meds that are doing it to him, Hannah."

CHAPTER 20

H annah pulled the wide strap of the purple linen bag over her shoulder. "If I have to see Evan and his baby mama every time I go to the farmers market, I'd better get used to it," she said bravely and glanced at Alex.

It was ridiculous that she, a middle-aged librarian who'd been married for ten years, should feel shy looking at an attractive man who may or may not be aware of the things he'd said last night. Her marriage was over, after all. Her ex had left her for another. She was no longer bound by her vows because they meant nothing to the man who had slipped the ring on her finger.

Always have, always will.

All night, the words had played on repeat in her mind.

I see you, Hannah Banana. No matter the eyes.

"Right." Alex crossed his hands behind his head and nodded encouragement. "And if you need me to come and have a word with Evan about being a total douche, let me know. Happy to oblige."

"Hmm." It was a chivalrous offer, but there was nothing left of last night's softness in his wry voice. Deciding it was safe, Hannah went over to the corner of the

bookstore where Alex was sitting in his cozy armchair. The morning sun was shining through the window, and the sweet, muted light lit up the corner. He
was dressed in an army T-shirt and gray sweatpants,
his hair still disheveled from sleeping.

She put her hands on either one of the armrests
and leaned over him.

"What are you doing?" Alex pressed his head into
the back of the chair, dropping his hands by his side.

It only made her feel even safer. Hannah studied
his face. Did he remember last night? "How is your
eye?" she asked finally. "Why are you wearing the
patch?"

"Habit. Uh—old habits die hard."

Slowly, she reached out and took the eye patch
off. He didn't resist, his eyes gripping the arms of his
chair. "Is the light too bright?" she asked.

"No."

She leaned in closer. "I can see the stitches."

"Oh God. Please don't remind me." Alex drew in a
raspy breath. "To tell you the truth, I can't get myself
to look at it. I'll get sick. What does it look like?"

She smiled. "It looks like a star. You have a star in
your eye, Alex."

"Is it hideous?"

"No. It's...just a star pattern around your iris."

He swallowed, his gaze holding hers. "Hannah..."

She tipped her head. "Yes?"

"Last night..."

"No." Hannah put a finger on his lips, and then, slowly, deliberately, she kissed the finger between their mouths.

Alex watched as she rose and straightened the bag. "When are you coming back?" His voice shook as he exhaled.

"Soon." She turned away. "I'll bring you something yummy for breakfast." He didn't reply. When she glanced back over her shoulder, his starry eyes were on her.

She smiled. "That was for last night," she said and walked to the door. "Now we're even."

"What happened last night? Hannah—come back. What happened last night?" Alex asked, his voice rising in tone with his urgency.

"You don't remember?" Her smile deepening, Hannah left the bookstore, stepping out into the warm, bright sunshine. She'd seen it in his eyes—he remembered. He just didn't know if he remembered everything. And now it was his turn to stew and wonder and imagine things.

Unless Hannah was wrong. Then Alex would be quite confused right now. But, a small, naughty corner of her brain hoped, still imagining things.

The air was still cool from the night, but there was no wind ruffling the ocean. The water lay still, shimmering like a rare blue pearl in the rugged clamshell of the cliffs.

To warm up, Hannah walked quickly. It was hard not to think about Alex. And even though she was no longer obliged to be faithful to Evan, kissing Alex still seemed illegal. It *felt* amazing, even with a finger guarding their lips—but forbidden. Whether she wanted or not, Hannah was still married. And even if her husband didn't honor his promises and didn't care about hers, Hannah was not like him. She didn't want to be. She needed a clean break, a divorce, a stamp and a seal confirming she was out.

Squelching the fluttering in her stomach that came from the breakneck speed of changes in her life, Hannah hitched her bag higher and quickened her pace. What was the right thing to do when one was falling for a good man but still married to a bad one? How many feelings could her heart hold? How many secrets fit in her soul?

The farmers market was in full swing when she arrived. Hannah joined the gathering crowd, more than ready for the loud buzz of talking and laughter and busyness to distract her mind.

Rows of cheerful farm stalls greeted the early risers, most of them offering freshly harvested fruits and vegetables. Hannah strolled past them in the warming morning light, letting the flow of market-goers carry her along as she admired the crisp apples, ripe strawberries, and plump tomatoes beckoning from woven baskets and wooden trays. The local florist had a table full of pretty glass vases with luscious, fragrant bouquets bursting with color, and Hannah was sorely tempted to buy herself a floral treat.

But she didn't have money to spare, so she drifted on to find a baker. Here and there she stopped at stands showcasing treasures, from whimsical carved wooden sculptures to ceramics and watercolor paintings, and chatted with the local artisans.

A group of children skipped past Hannah, sugar pastries and mason jars full of lemonade in their hands. She changed course to go where they'd come from, and after only a few steps, the scent of freshly baked bread told her that she was on the right track. When she found the bakery truck, she got in line. Each customer took their time when it was their turn, carefully selecting their goods and chatting with the elderly baker.

"And what can I get you?" he asked Hannah when it was her turn.

"A dozen rolls, please," she said politely. She had a feeling that Beth and Sara would stop by sometime during the morning to see how Alex was doing. "And two almond croissants with powdered sugar, please."

"Only two?" The baker laughed at her request, but it was a kind laugh, the way a parent laughed when a kid said something unexpected. He shook open a big brown paper bag and picked up long wooden tongs to pick the rolls. "Are you new in town?"

"Sort of." Hannah smiled, delighted that, like the other locals, she, too, got to chat with the jolly baker. "I grew up here, but my mom moved to San Jose when I was ten. I only just returned."

"Ah. And who is your mom?"

"Her name is Sue Banner," Hannah said. "Do you know her?"

"Sue? Sue?" the baker murmured. "Curls like yours?"

"Yes. Only she's blond."

He nodded, picking the rolls with care. "Maybe. Maybe I know Sue Banner. Tell her Miguel Martinez says hi. And when you do, listen to her response." Smiling, he put the paper bag on the counter. "Next time you need rolls, tell me what she said. I'd like to know." He picked up another bag and pulled out the sheet with freshly baked croissants.

"Sure." Hannah smiled back. "But just so you know—being brutally honest is her trademark."

"Now I'm sure it's her." Miguel laughed. "Make sure to let me know." He put the two requested croissants in the bag and added it to the rolls on the counter. Then he set a raspberry square on a piece of wax paper and handed it to her, the way bakers and butchers handed little children treats to sweeten the time while their parents shopped. "This one's for you, young lady. Because you have your mother's eyes. And even more because I'm glad you stopped by. Welcome back to Mendocino Beach, huh?"

"Oh." Hannah smiled and took the ruby-red, sweet-smelling pastry. "Thank you. I'll be back to report what Mom says." She paid for her purchases, then stowed the bread in her bag and wandered on, buying homemade peach and currant jams, a small log of goat cheese with honey-glazed walnuts, small garden cucumbers, and plump tomatoes. The rolls were fresh from the oven, perfectly crusty on the outside and without a doubt soft and chewy on the inside. As Hannah walked on, she was picturing the delicious brunch she and Alex would have when she got back to the bookstore.

Lost in thought, she bit into her raspberry square. The buttery layers of the dough melted in her mouth, and the topping was perfectly sweet and refreshingly fruity.

A woman smiled at Hannah in passing and indicated her own upper lip. Hannah smiled back a thanks for the sisterly heads-up and wiped the powdered sugar off her lips.

"Uh...Hannah? Hannah!"

She stopped. The voice calling her name was breathless with stress, hesitant, and unfamiliar. And yet, Hannah knew immediately who was calling.

CHAPTER 21

"Hannah? Hi," the woman called again.

Running wouldn't solve anything. It was a pity because that's exactly what Hannah wanted to do. Instead, she slowly turned around.

The pregnant Allison stood behind her, fingers knotted into a nervous ball. "Hi," she said quickly. "Can we talk?"

It took a moment before Hannah's brain caught up to the situation. Then she said, "What do you want to say to me?"

"I want to say...I didn't know he was married."

"You didn't know." Hannah's eyes searched the younger woman's face for signs that she was lying. It was unpleasant because the pretty features automatically brought up images of Evan gazing lovingly into those eyes, Evan kissing that mouth, Evan caressing that cheek.

Allison shook her head. When she spoke, the words tumbled from her lips. "He said he was single. He said his company's headquarters were in San Jose, so he had to spend most of his time there. He told me not to come to San Jose because he didn't want to run into a jealous ex and that we should spend all of our time in San Francisco. Once I went anyway, just to surprise him with a nice lunch, but he really was working in an office and was annoyed with me for interrupting his workday. I didn't visit again. I thought we just had a...a normal long-distance relationship."

"Really?" It wasn't meant sarcastically, but all of Hannah's doubts weighed down the word.

"Really. When we met last time, it was a total shock." Allison's hand went protectively to her belly. "I swear, Hannah. I always thought I was a smart cookie, but I'm actually pretty dim. I had no idea he was seeing someone else, let alone that he was married! *Married*!" The angry frown pulling on her eyebrows wasn't for Hannah, but for the man who had fooled her.

"Well." Hannah couldn't help but believe Allison. But that didn't mean she nursed any warm feelings for the other woman. "I suppose it doesn't matter much to you. You have my husband, his baby, and, I understand, my mother's house." She flushed warm when she said the words. Hannah didn't like conflict, never had, and this was the harshest thing she'd ever said to a stranger.

"I didn't move into that house," Allison said quickly. "I didn't even unpack my car. I arrived in town the day we met, and I didn't stay the night."

Hannah stared at her. All this time, she'd pictured the woman in her bedroom, in Evan's arms. "You didn't stay?"

"No! No, of course I didn't. Luckily, I didn't quit my job for that...for..." She swallowed, and her second hand joined the first in cradling her belly. "Evan. Your husband." A tense breath escaped her, and she shifted her weight. Beads of sweat trickled down her temples, and she wiped them away.

"Here." Hannah stepped into the shade of the honey stand awning. The sun was climbing quickly higher in the spotless azure of the sky, and there was still no sea breeze to relieve the rising temperature. "Come out of the sun. It's too hot."

Gratefully, Allison followed Hannah into the shade.

"What did Evan say about Mendocino Beach?" Hannah asked.

"He told me to come here. That he'd bought a house and wanted me to live here with him. That the school was great and the town safe." She shaded her eyes and looked out at the happy, milling crowd. "I actually came up here before to check it out. I didn't tell him because I didn't want him to come and change my mind. I loved the town the moment I saw it."

"Um." Hannah scratched her arm. She was at a loss. "How old are you, Allison?"

"I'm thirty-two." Allison smiled an uncertain smile. "And you?"

"Older than that. So you just up and left for Mendocino Beach?"

"Yep." Allison shook her head as if she still couldn't believe she'd done that. "I work remotely, and I love this little town. I thought moving here was a great idea."

"And what are you planning to do now?"

Allison looked Hannah fully in the eye. "I only have a plan for today. And that was to talk to you, and to apologize for my stupidity. I honestly didn't know he was lying to me all these years. Maybe I should have figured it out." She looked down at her belly and shifted her weight again, clearly uncomfortable. "But I didn't. I don't have a suspicious mind."

"Same." The word escaped Hannah before she could stop herself. Then she sighed. There were just a few too many parallels between Allison's story and her own to stay angry with the woman. "Same, Allison. I should have put it together too, but I'm not a suspicious person either."

A small smile tugged at the corners of Allison's lip. Again she reached up and wiped the sweat off her temples. "I understand if you're angry with me. You are his wife. I didn't want to break up your marriage. And I'm truly sorry for what happened."

"Evan is the one who broke up our marriage," Hannah said slowly. "Not you, not me. That man did it all by his lying lonesome."

Allison looked up, a grateful expression on her pale face. "Thank you, Hannah," she said. "I know this isn't easy."

"It's not." Hannah bit her lip, wavering on how much talking was too much. But the topic of Allison's pregnancy still felt like such an obvious elephant in the room. "We tried to get pregnant for a long time, you know. That was... It's not easy."

Allison closed her eyes. "I hate him," she said through gritted teeth. "I was just his...breeding cow."

"Oh! Oh." Hannah's eyes widened at Allison's knee-jerk anger, which was so different from her own reaction. She'd lain awake last night, trying to find what was left of her love for Evan. But the connection was gone. The man she'd thought she married didn't exist. Maybe he had never existed.

Hannah exhaled, letting go and setting Evan free. Then she took a deep breath, filling her lungs with a new beginning, and said, "I hope that's not true, Allison. I hope you two like each other better than that. You're going to have a child together."

"Maybe Evan is the dad. But lucky for me, we aren't married. Oops." She pressed her fingertips to her mouth. "Sorry. I'm sorry."

"It's okay. I know what you mean. But that's for the two of you to work out. Good luck." Hannah couldn't get involved in the child-situation. Her own back-story around the topic was too painful, and besides, it was none of her business. "Listen, I'd better go."

"Thanks for stopping and letting me talk to you." Allison suddenly looked impossibly young. "You have no idea how much I wish I'd never met him." Regret swiped like a cloud over her face.

"Thanks for stopping me and taking the trouble of explaining." Hannah was already turning to leave, but something in the other woman's voice made her stop again. "You're about to have the baby, aren't you?" she said, her voice softer than before. "Are you going to be all right?"

Allison nodded, but her face was even paler than before. Now the sweat didn't just pearl on her temples, but on her forehead too, and her brown eyes looked huge and dark in her face.

Hannah took a step toward her. "Are you all right? You look like you're about to faint."

"It *hurts*," Allison whispered and gripped the awning pole beside her to steady herself. "I think I'm having contractions." She frowned at her belly, and her eyes widened even more. "Hannah? What—is that?"

Hannah's eyes darted to Allison's skirt where a dark blotch was spreading quickly, staining the delicate fabric. She gasped, covering her mouth with a hand, and set her bags down. "Allison! Please tell me it's not what it looks like. You're just having a little accident, aren't you?"

Allison shook her head, her expression scared as she met Hannah's gaze. "I'm not doing anything!" she replied, her voice trembling. She swayed slightly, prompting Hannah to grasp her arm for support. Helpless, the younger woman looked up. "It's too early for the baby to come!"

"Hey, are you two okay over there? Do you want to sample the clover honey?" The beekeeper craned his head over a towering stack of clear plastic boxes filled with honeycomb.

"Do you have a chair?" Hannah's voice rose with stress as she put an arm around Allison's unwieldy waist. "Can she sit down, please?"

On cue, Allison hissed in pain and grasped her cramping belly.

"Here. Here." The beekeeper hastened around the display, bringing his own wooden stool. "Sit, lady. She's going to faint!"

"Your water broke, Allison." Hannah sounded calm, though panic was spreading like wildfire inside her. "We need to get you to the hospital." She looked up to the beekeeper. "Can you take care of her for a while so I can get my car? It's going to take me twenty minutes or so."

"No! Hannah, don't leave me, please!" Allison gasped. "It really hurts!"

"Ah, no, no, no, you've got to stay with your friend! I can't... Listen, I'm going to call an ambulance," the beekeeper said quickly. "Who knows how quickly the baby wants to come! She said she was early, didn't she? Don't even risk getting stuck in traffic. You don't want to deliver it at the side of the road, do you?" With shaking hands, he pulled out his phone and tapped on the screen.

Her raw nerves made Hannah nervously laugh out loud. "Wish I knew how to do that!"

Allison groaned as another contraction came on. "I'm supposed to have another month to get back home!"

"That may no longer be an option." Hannah squeezed Allison's trembling fingers. The thought of an ambulance was reassuring. She had never taken a maternity class and frankly, had no idea what she was supposed to do. "Did they tell you what to do, Alli? What do we do?"

CHAPTER 22

A passing family stopped beside them, the mother's brow knitted in concern. "You go on, David," she told her husband and wiggled the baby out of her carrier. "Take the kids and go ahead. I'll catch up later." Her husband took one look at Allison's pained expression, blanched, snatched the baby from his wife's arms, and herded their toddler off with promises of sweets and lemonade.

"Did your water break?" The woman put a hand on Allison's shoulder.

Allison's eyes closed, and she gritted her teeth as she arched her back.

"Yes, it just broke." Hannah was grateful for the woman's competent tone. At least she'd *had* a baby... "Please help us. It's her first, it's early, and I have no idea what to do."

"You're all right. Can you drive her to the hospital?" the woman asked.

"The ambulance is on its way." The beekeeper had retreated back behind his table, warily peeking over his stacked honeycomb.

"Let's time her contractions. By the way, I'm Kirsten, and I'm a nurse. Cardiology, usually." She smiled and pulled out a phone, setting it to the stopwatch. "And you two are...?"

"Her name is Allison. I'm Hannah." Prompted, Hannah remembered that contractions needed to be timed, though she had no clue how to do it.

"Uh-oh." Kirsten looked up. "They're pretty close. How long have you had them?"

"All morning, but not this hard! I thought they were just those practice contractions, you know, the Braxton Hicks ones," Allison murmured, her tense shoulders relaxing as she sank once more back onto her stool. "Please, tell me this isn't really happening," she pleaded, desperation in her words. "My mother was supposed to be with me. She's in Greece—she was barely going to make it back for the due date!"

"Then your friend will have to do." Kirsten smiled at Hannah, who nodded awkwardly. "And when your mom gets here, you'll be sitting pretty and picture-perfect on your sofa, showing off your happy, healthy baby."

"I hear a siren—there's the ambulance." Relief flooded Hannah as she spotted the vehicle. "Hold out just a bit longer, Alli. You're going to be fine."

During the next, long contraction, two EMTs arrived and helped Allison onto a stretcher. Kristen informed them about the rapid contractions and offered her well wishes before heading off to find her family.

Allison turned to Hannah. "Are you coming with me? I know it's a lot to ask—but I don't want to be alone. I'm scared."

Hannah had too much adrenaline in her system to think clearly. But how could she say no? It seemed cruel to let Alli face this alone.

"Hop on in, then," the EMT said, waving her into the ambulance. "The nearest hospital is in Mendocino Cove and I'd rather the doctor delivers the baby." He turned to Allison. "Not that I can't do it. I totally can. My name is Hans, by the way."

"Oh." Allison threw Hannah a desperate look. "Please? Don't leave me alone."

Before Hannah could think it over, she climbed into the ambulance and strapped herself in on the spare seat, Hans closed the door, and off they went. With practiced movements, Hans attached a pulse oximeter to Alli's finger and placed a blood pressure cuff on her arm.

"Do you have a hospital bag?" Hannah asked to distract Alli. Even she knew about the bags full of nightgowns and lanolin creams, hair ties and crackers that absolutely needed to be packed and ready by the door.

"I do."

"Where is it?"

"In my car." Alli's face distorted in pain.

"Breathe," Hans said mildly. "Breathe like you learned in class."

Allison blew out a breath through pursed lips and relaxed again. "Oof."

Hannah braced herself for saying his name. "Does Evan have your car?"

"No." Alli shook her head. "I told you. I left him. After what he's done, we're over."

Hannah tipped her head to the side. "Then where are you staying? Where's your car?"

"It's parked near the harbor," Alli said. "The keys are in my purse. I rented a sublet over the laundromat."

Hannah chewed on the inside corner of her lips. "Is that where you're going to live with the baby?"

Alli shook her head. "It's only until I find something in San Francisco."

Hannah pulled over Alli's purse and searched for the keys, shoving them in her pocket. "So that's your plan, huh?" she said gently.

Alli's face scrunched up as if she was ready to cry. "My *plan* was to move into the beautiful seaside house my boyfriend bought for us. He was supposed to drive me to the hospital. He was supposed to help me change diapers at night. He was supposed to book a spot in a good preschool." She took a shuddering breath. "My plan went *poof*, Hannah, when I found out about you. And I'm supposed to have four more weeks to regroup!"

"All right, I get it. It'll be okay." Hannah took Alli's hand in hers. "Evan messed up both of our plans pretty good, didn't he?"

"Yeah." Alli squeezed Hannah's hand, tears in her eyes. "I'm going to get him," she whispered. "Just you wait and see, Hannah. I'm going to get him for this."

"Sheesh," Hans muttered. "Let's just... I mean, let's just all relax for now and get this baby out. Okay?"

"I have to make a call, Alli." Hannah leaned back. "I'll ask a friend to bring your bag to the hospital." She dialed Beth's number, told her in a few sentences what had happened, and asked her to meet at the hospital in Mendocino Cove.

"Sure," Beth said. "By the way, Sara's with me at the café; her boss told her to take the day off because they just won a major case. We're leaving as soon as we can. Hang in there."

Grateful for her friends, Hannah ended the call. "Alli," she said as she tucked it back into her purse. "Do you want me to call Evan and tell him to come to the hospital?"

"Are you kidding me?" Alli exhaled a breath the way a dragon exhaled fire. "I won't have that man anywhere near me."

"But..." Hannah couldn't believe she was going to say this, but it needed saying. "Alli, he's still the father."

"He can't be present at the birth if she doesn't want him," Hans said calmly, glancing at a monitor that was beeping alarmingly fast.

"I don't want him, Hannah." Alli was crying. "I don't trust him, and I really don't want him to watch me give birth!"

"Okay." Hannah patted her hand. "I thought I'd offer to call, but you sort it out between the two of you. It's none of my business."

The siren sounded again as the ambulance navigated crossroads, then it slowed and stopped. "Here we go." Hans jumped up and unclipped the monitors from Alli. The door opened, and the driver appeared, helping Hannah climb out.

Moments later, she found herself hurrying after Alli as they rolled her stretcher into the labor and delivery room.

"Are you going to wait outside?" Alli asked, with a last look at Hannah.

Hannah nodded a promise. "I'll just dip down to hand over your keys so we can get your hospital bag. Good luck! Everything will be fine."

The doors closed before she finished the sentence. She stood staring at it, and then she slumped into one of the chairs along the wall, closed her eyes, and let her head drop back in her neck. "Evan," she murmured, "you total and utter fool. I want to call you and tell you to get your butt over here, but now I can't even do that."

As if triggered by the thought, her phone vibrated. When she glanced at the screen, she saw that Beth and Sara had arrived and were in the cafeteria.

"Excuse me." She stopped a nurse hurrying out of the room. "Is she all right? Can I leave for a few minutes?"

"She's all right." The nurse smiled and said, "Go get yourself coffee and a piece of cake, but don't order a real big lunch. She's pretty far along. Good job getting her here in time."

Hannah thanked the nurse and made her way downstairs to the cafeteria. It was housed in a welcoming, open space with lots of light and large, potted plants to soften the corners. Doctors, patients, staff, and visitors sat together, eating and chatting. Outside the wide windows, a patio with white Adirondack chairs led to a lawn where a few patients and staff walked.

"Hannah! Over here!" Beth and Sara were already seated at a table, waving to her. "We got you tea and cake!" Sara whisper-yelled across the room. Smiling with relief to see the two, Hannah made her way to them and fell into an empty chair.

"Well," Beth said, smiling back. "Of all the pregnant women to drive to the hospital, did you have to pick this one?"

"Tell me about it." Hannah shook her head, feeling dazed. "I cannot believe that just happened."

"It's fate," Sara said in a foggy, mysterious voice that made her sound like the local wise woman. "You and Allison now have a bond for life."

CHAPTER 23

Y eah, right." Hannah picked up the cup of tea Beth pushed toward her. "Talking about that—Allison told me not to call my dear husband and father of her child."

"Is that a good idea?" Beth asked, concern in her voice.

"It's up to her," Hannah replied softly. "She said she left him. The last couple of days, she stayed in some stranger's apartment. But she can't go back there with a baby."

"Oh dear."

"And she said she'd have Evan thrown out if he came." Hannah glanced at the cake on the table, suddenly feeling ravenous. "Can I?" she asked, pointing at the dessert.

"Of course," Sara said and pushed the tray over to her. "I got us raspberry, lemon, and chocolate marble cheesecake. Take whichever you like."

Hannah selected the lemon cheesecake, while Sara opted for chocolate and Beth claimed the raspberry. Hungry, Hannah piled a bit of cake and whipped cream on her fork and savored the first bite. "Hmm," she murmured, surprised. "So creamy and light and refreshing! It's just a touch tart but perfectly sweet as well."

The black tea Beth poured now was good too, sweet and milky, at that perfect temperature where it was cool enough to be easy to drink but still hot enough to warm her insides.

Hannah drank thirstily, and when she set down the cup, a happy sigh escaped her. "I think I was in shock until now," she admitted, feeling the tension in her shoulders melt away. "That's not how I pictured my morning."

Sara set her fork down, her expression serious. "I think Evan should know," she said quietly. "It's his child too. I can understand not letting him in the room while she's giving birth. She should do whatever she wants there. But to not tell him at all?"

"Trust is a privilege," Beth interjected, her tone somber. She had barely touched her cake. "He lost hers."

"And mine," Hannah added, a hint of sadness in her voice.

"And yours," Beth agreed, patting Hannah's arm gently. "Where is Allison's family?"

Hannah needed a moment to remember. "Her mother is on a sailing trip. There doesn't seem to be any other family."

"Evan has to be told," Sara repeated. "He knows she'll have the baby at some point soon. What's Allison's plan here? If nothing else, she'll need Evan's financial support."

Hannah reached for Beth's cheesecake to finish it. "I don't think she has a plan." She lifted her head just in time to catch Beth and Sara exchange a glance. "What?" she asked, her cheeks full of rich cheesecake and fresh raspberry topping. "What does that look mean?"

"Do *you* have a plan, honey?" Beth asked gently. "Or are you planning on living in Alex's apartment forever?"

Hannah swallowed, feeling caught out. "No?"

"No," Beth said gently.

"But we're not talking about me." Hannah wiped her mouth. "And Alli asked me to stay with her. I should probably be there when she wants me."

"Alli?" Sara smiled. "Are you two on a nickname basis?"

"I suppose we are. I mean, her water broke in front of me. There's a certain bonding potential."

"So go, keep her company." Beth rummaged in her purse and handed Hannah a car key. "I drove my car, and Sara drove hers. She has to get back to pick up the kids. We'll see you later."

"Thank you. Um, if I'm not going back with you—how do I get back to Mendocino Beach?" Hannah took the keys.

"You take Beth's blue Honda Hatchback whenever you're ready. She'll leave it for you and come back in Alli's car to swap, and then you can take Alli's car when you want to come home." Sara rose. "When they're ready to leave, you might give Alli and the baby a ride," she added. "She won't be able to drive herself home, and it doesn't sound like she'll let Evan do the honors."

"Right." Hannah clutched the keys. "And if I do that—where exactly do I bring Alli and the baby? She can't go back into the sublet. Where is her home?"

The three women exchanged looks. "Excellent question," Sara said finally. "Beth?"

"Beats me." Beth shrugged helplessly. "Her mother's place?"

"I'll figure it out," Hannah murmured. There had to be someone. Friends?

She rose to return the cafeteria dishes when the double-wide door swung open. The friendly nurse from Alli's room peeked in, and when she spotted Hannah, she waved for her to come.

"Go." Beth took the tray from her, and Hannah rushed over.

"Your sister wants you." Smiling, the nurse held the door open. "Congratulations, auntie! It's a beautiful baby boy!"

Hannah was too flustered to correct the nurse. "A baby boy? Is Alli okay?" She followed the nurse, who had already turned back toward the staircase.

"Mama is doing well. Baby is a little on the early side," the nurse reported as they took the steps two at a time. "You'd best talk to Doctor Summers."

It wasn't the news Hannah expected. Somehow, as soon as the ambulance had shown up, she'd assumed the baby would be just fine and that she'd return to a happy, fat little baby, nursing in Alli's arms.

Her heart started to pump faster as she hurried after the nurse.

CHAPTER 24

At the door, the nurse congratulated Hannah again and left to help a colleague. Hannah took a moment to brace herself, and then she knocked. There was no response, so she cracked it open.

A doctor in a white lab coat looked up from a chart.

"I'm Hannah," she whispered. "Here for Alli?"

"Oh, come in. I'm Dr. Summers." He smiled. "Allison asked for you. She's doing great."

"Hey. Congratulations, Alli!"

Alli was lying in the freshly made bed, her face drawn with exhaustion. "Hannah, he's early." Her lips trembled, and she pressed them into a white line. "They took Tommy."

"They took him...where?" Every atom in Hannah wanted the baby to be all right. Nothing else mattered.

Calmly, the doctor put down his tablet and slipped the stylus into his breast pocket. "Tommy went to visit our special care nursery. It's really mostly precaution, but his lungs need a moment to catch up. I promise they will."

"Hannah—can you go to him? Can you have a look, make sure he's okay?" Alli begged. "I just need to know he's okay."

"I think that's a great idea." The doctor nodded encouragement at Hannah. "Why don't you go and take some photos for Mom? She'll be up and about soon enough, but it was a first birth, and a very fast one at that." He smiled at Alli. "I'd like you to rest a little to make sure there's no more bleeding. Tomorrow we'll get you a wheelchair, and you can go see your baby yourself."

"Yeah." Alli nodded, pale and resigned. "Thanks, Dr. Summers. It's not that I don't believe he's taken care of. It's just..."

"I understand; it's different when the family has an eye on the little ones. Don't worry. Your sister is here for you." He turned to Hannah. "If you like, you can stay the night. We have cots."

"Thank you. Um." Hannah went to stand by Alli. "Can I just have a quick word alone?"

"Yes, of course." Dr. Summers went to the door. "Well done, Allison," he said. "Let the nurse know if you need anything. I'll check in again in an hour." He left the two women alone.

"Can you please go now and make sure Tommy is okay?" Allison took Hannah's hand. "I really need to know they didn't accidentally switch him up, or... I don't know. I know it's irrational, but I just really need someone by his side."

"Of course I will." Hannah patted Alli's hand. "But, Alli..." She wiped a strand of hair out of the younger woman's face. "Maybe I shouldn't be the one sitting with him tonight, or tomorrow, or however long it will take for the two of you to heal."

"No. I know. I'm sorry to ask you all of this." A big fat tear dripped from Alli's left eye and ran down her cheek. "I wish my mom could be here!"

"Ah! Hormones. I've heard about this." Hannah smiled and pulled a tissue from the box on the night-stand, drying Alli's tears. "It's not that. I'll stay as long as you want me with your cute baby and consider it a treat. But Tommy has a dad. You might let Evan know that you need help. He should help you and your baby."

"I *hate* Evan!" Alli's brow dropped. "He totally be-trayed me. And his son!"

"Yes, I know. And you don't have to love him ever again. You don't have to get back together; you don't have to do anything. But this is not about your feel-ings, Alli. It's about your baby. Tommy needs him *now*. Evan should be the one to sit with his baby and make sure he's okay. At least while you're healing? Let him take care of his son when you can't."

Alli's eyes glittered angrily. "You're one to talk, Hannah." She pulled her hand away. "You allow him to take your mother's house without saying a single word."

"I'll get a lawyer."

Alli looked up. "If you get one, I'll get one too."

Hannah smiled. "There you go. Ask Evan to come to the hospital and help. You can't heal when you're worried about your baby."

"Okay." Alli was crying again, and Hannah got more tissues. "But can you go check on Tommy now?"

"Yes." Hannah went to the door, torn between staying and drying Alli's tears and checking on the baby. "You call your baby daddy, and I make sure your baby isn't alone until he gets here."

"Deal," Alli said and blew her nose. "Thank you."

Hannah left, sincerely hoping that she had done the right thing. It didn't feel good to meddle in Alli's affairs, but Evan couldn't just lie and cheat and then claim his heir in eighteen years. He needed to fix the mess he'd caused. Including sitting with his baby son and helping Alli raise him, whatever that arrangement looked like.

The same nurse who'd fetched her earlier brought Hannah to the special care nursery. The light was dimmed, and the room was silent but for the quiet humming of machines. "We only have two babies right now," she said with a smile as she brought Hannah over to an incubator unit. "Tommy and a sweet little preemie girl. Tommy is over here, and there's a chair, if you want to sit."

Hannah approached the incubator, her heart fluttered with a mixture of anticipation and apprehension. She couldn't help but feel a wave of concern for Alli's newborn baby in this clinical environment.

Peering through the transparent walls of the incubator, she saw a small bundle—all red skin and puckered lips—nestled amid a tangle of wires and tubes and surrounded by softly glowing monitors.

Hannah was struck by how tiny and fragile Tommy looked. A surge of empathy washed over her as she thought of Alli's longing to hold him.

Gently, Hannah reached for her phone and snapped a photo that she texted Alli, and then she carried a plastic chair over to the incubator. "I'm here, Tommy," she whispered, putting a hand on the incubator. "You're not alone, sweetheart."

She had started humming a lullaby when Alli texted back. *Thank you, Hannah. Evan's in San Jose but on his way. Will take a few hours...*

CHAPTER 25

"Alex?" Sara stepped into the bookstore and let the door shut behind her.

Alex was sitting behind the counter. He was wearing his eyepatch again. His good eye was intensely blue and curious. "Sara." He rose. "Do you have news?"

"The baby has arrived." Sara went to the counter. "Hannah stayed to help Alli."

He nodded slowly. "How are mom and baby?"

"Hannah just texted. Mom is sleeping. The baby was a little early, and they're making sure his lungs are going to be okay. They're keeping an eye on him for now."

Alex crossed his arms. "Hannah had a long day."

Sara had called Alex earlier, to catch him up on the marketplace events. "That's true." She smiled. "She's had a cup of milk tea and two slices of cheesecake with fruit. Beth and I did what we could."

"Hmm." Impassively, Alex looked at her. "Why didn't she come back to Mendocino Beach with you?"

Sara folded her hands. "Because Alli asked her to stay with the baby in the nursery until Evan comes. Why are you wearing the eye patch?"

"Force of habit."

"Did my book on patterns come in?"

He dropped his arms. "Not yet. I'll call when it does."

She tipped her head—she didn't like the way Alex looked. "Hey. Are you all right? You look pale."

He touched his jaw. "That's the life and lot of a bookstore owner."

She narrowed her eyes at him. "I'll just have a quick look around the new book section. I want to buy Andy a little something for standing him up when his parents came for dinner."

"Sure." He sat back down and picked up his thriller.

"Oo-kay." Sara went to where Alex put the new arrivals. Her mind was churning. Alex was acting strange. And why would he wear that eye patch again? Was the sunlight hurting his eye?

Her thoughts elsewhere, she turned to walk down the aisle where the arts and crafts section was.

"Hoopla!" A tall man turned just in time to step aside. "Careful there!"

"Ah!" Sara's hands flew to her throat. "Mr. Sterling!"

Her boss blinked. "Sara. What are you...?" He looked left and right over her head, as if more middle-aged lady would jump at him. "What are you doing here?"

"I'm so sorry." Sara smiled, a little unnerved. "I didn't see you there."

He made a small sound in the back of his throat to acknowledge her apology. Then he returned his attention to the shelf with historical non-fiction. "I didn't know you were a reader, Sara. What's your preferred genre?"

"Um." Longingly, she peered at the arts and crafts section. She had to pass her boss to get to it, and the aisles between the shelves were narrow. "I like to draw, actually. I'm here for the...those." She pointed.

"Oh. Forgive me." He stepped back from the books he was browsing to give her space to pass.

It had been a while since Sara had counted calories. She liked her luscious curves though Andy had made sounds about dieting and exercising, eating more protein and fewer carbs. Maybe she should've listened. Being a stick would come in handy right about now.

Sara held her breath, trying to make herself as skinny as possible.

What she'd forgotten was that holding her breath inflated her already blessed chest.

"Pardon me," she murmured and squished by, accidentally brushing her boss. Flames shot into her cheeks.

"No problem," Mr. Sterling replied, his gaze drifting upward as if searching for escape from the uncomfortable moment. "Are you where you need to be?"

The only way forward was to pretend it never happened. "Yes. Thank you." Sara squatted down, too embarrassed to look at Sterling and cursing Alex yet again for putting the craft books so near the ground. There were no new books she wanted; she'd seen that with a glance. But after squeezing by so dramatically, she needed to spend time looking.

After a moment, she realized Mr. Sterling had pulled out a book about the Roman Empire and was engrossed in it.

"Um." Sara rose, unsure how to exit the situation gracefully. "I suppose there's nothing for me today."

Mr. Sterling looked up from his book, surprising her with a genuine smile. It was a departure from his usual absent-minded demeanor, and Sara found herself momentarily taken aback.

"I wonder..." he said, his tone thoughtful.

Sara nodded, but then she tilted her head in question. "What?" She forced herself not to stare at his smiling lips. "What do you wonder?"

"Well—it's your day off, and far be it from me to...but I'm wondering whether you'd like to get coffee. With me. My treat, I mean."

"With you." Sara blinked in surprise at her boss's unexpected invitation. It was clear he wasn't asking her out romantically but extending a friendly gesture. Probably because of the Snyder case.

"It's a beautiful afternoon, and a new beach bistro opened up yesterday. I've never been over there, but I thought I might go. Support the business, you know."

Sara nodded. The entire town was invested in making the bistro a success. It was a treat to walk along the sandy beach to the little restaurant and have a bite to eat before returning.

"Sure," she replied. "Sounds good. I want to support the bistro too."

Mr. Sterling's smile widened at her acceptance and politely, he gestured for Sara to lead the way. "Would you like to walk?" he asked as he opened the door for her. "Or should we drive?"

Sara threw a longing glance at the sea. It was impossibly blue, rippling with tiny glittering waves. A long line of pelicans cruised by, and a gull on top of the bookstore screamed at them. "It's been a while since I walked on the beach."

"I agree." He went to a car parked at the curb and opened it, setting the history book he'd bought on the back seat. "Should we drive to the harbor and start there?"

"Sure." Sara watched as Mr. Sterling walked around the car to open the door for her. "Um. Thank you."

The car, a sleek Mercedes with leather seats and a futuristic dashboard, felt like a world away from their usual environment. Sara strapped herself in and folded her hands in her lap, trying to shake off the awkwardness of the situation.

She'd never once interacted with the man outside the office. In fact, Mr. Sterling was close to a perfect stranger, despite the fact that Sara arranged his dispositions.

"So," she began, breaking the silence as Mr. Sterling shifted the stick into first gear and pulled away from the curb. Despite the heat outside, the car's interior remained pleasantly cool. "What's that book you got?"

"It's a historical account of senate meetings." He accelerated, and the momentum pressed Sara into her seat.

"The Roman Empire, huh?"

"Boring, I know. I'm putting a case together and want to make a certain point."

"Ah." Sara couldn't imagine a senate meeting in ancient Rome being relevant in court.

"Yes. How was your day so far?" Already, they'd reached the harbor. What would've been a twenty-minute walk from the bookstore had barely been the blink of an eye. "Calm and quiet?"

"Well, not exactly."

He glanced at her, one hand on the door. "What happened?"

For a moment, Sara hesitated. But she had committed to a half-hour walk together. They had to talk about more than the Roman Empire.

"So, my friend just moved to Mendocino Beach, and she's married to this *guy*." Sara fumbled with the unfamiliar mechanism to unbuckle her seatbelt. By the time she succeeded, Sterling had already circled around to her side. With a practiced motion, he opened the door, offering his hand to help Sara out of the car. "What guy?" he asked, interested.

CHAPTER 26

S ara took his hand. It was warm and firm and harder than she'd expected, the fingers that closed around hers those of a pianist. "His name is Evan," she said. "It's a long story. Once I start, you'll have to listen all the way to the end. Are you sure you want to know?" She let go and smoothed her wide linen pants.

"Yes, I do." He smiled. "I like stories."

"Me too." Pleased, Sara started walking toward the beach, telling him about Hannah, the house, and the baby.

Matching his pace to hers, Sterling listened thoughtfully, his eyebrows rising higher and higher. "Dear me," he said when Sara finished. "You were right. It's a whole story."

"Isn't it? By the way, I gave her your card."

"Well done." He smiled.

Smiling back, Sara slipped out of her sandals, feeling the warm sand under her feet, and set them on the step by the seawall. There were already other pairs of shoes, waiting for their owners to return. "You've never been to the bistro?"

"It's a first for me. You've gone before?"

Sara laughed. "Loads of times. Here's how it's done: take off your shoes and leave them here, then walk barefoot along the water line to the bistro. We'll have coffee and cake, and then we come back and pick up our shoes."

"I see." Mr. Sterling's dark eyes crinkled at the corners. "I wasn't aware there were rules. I'm rather used to wearing shoes in company."

Sara's gaze drifted downward to his leather shoes. "I'm afraid you can't," she said, a tone of mischief in her voice. "The saltwater is going to ruin these in no time."

"I don't want that." Smiling, Sterling sat on the sea-wall and removed his shoes and black socks, tucking them in his shoes and setting them next to Sara's sandals. "Good?"

"Good." She smiled back and nodded approval.

He glanced up at her, pointing at the slacks of his designer suit. "Fold up the legs, I suppose?"

"If you want to keep dry in the water." Sara inspected her own wide, airy pants. "I'd fold mine too, but they're linen. They won't stay up."

"Then we'll stay above the waterline," he decided and rose. "I once had a case where the plaintiff—Oh. No. No shop talk today. Tell me more about this Evan and your friend Hannah."

They started walking on the beach. The fine sand was warm and soft, washed clean by the receding tide, and the sea breeze tugged playfully on their hair and clothes.

Sara answered Sterling's question about the house, and what exactly Evan had said, and what exactly Hannah had done. Afterward, they talked more, about other things. By the time she'd explained to her boss which seashells to collect and which ones to toss, how to spot sea glass hidden in washed-up kelp, and what happened when tourists forgot to watch out for sneaker waves, they reached the beach bistro.

"Very cute!" Sara stopped to admire the newly reno-vated restaurant. "I like the blue paint. And the wooden deck is such a good idea!" Before, the outside tables and chairs had simply stood in the sand. While it was fun to bury one's toes in the sand, the chairs and tables had always shifted.

"I hope the umbrellas won't fly out of their bases and whack anyone." Stepping on the platform, Sterling threw a critical look at the large, off-white market um-brellas that shaded the patio. "That's a lawsuit waiting to happen."

"Surely not." Sara laughed. "They're pretty. I like them."

"Wherever you like!" a server called busily from the door.

"All right." Sterling pulled out a chair for her. "Please."

"Don't mind if I do." Smiling, Sara settled into the chair, taking in the idyllic scene around her—the glis-tening sea, the warmth of the sun, and the charming ambiance of the beach bistro.

It was a welcome change of pace, being able to en-gage in a long conversation about topics that interested her, all while enjoying a picturesque setting and having the attention of a gentleman. Maybe it was only for a brief, sunny afternoon. But Sara couldn't help but savor the moment.

"Just a second." Sterling went inside the bistro and reappeared a moment later with two laminated menu cards. He handed one to Sara and sat, studying his own. "How do you feel about a proper meal, Sara? I skipped lunch, and the walk has given me an appetite."

"That sounds lovely." Browsing the new and improved menu, the cheesecake at the hospital suddenly seemed a long time ago.

Sterling glanced at her over his menu. "What do you like?"

There was a variety of dishes, many more than the last bistro owner had offered. She chuckled. "Honestly, it all sounds so good. I can't decide."

"Hmm." He folded the card, placed it on the table, and a moment later, a teenage server arrived. "Hi. Do you serve Negroni?"

"Yep." The kid shook his hair out of his forehead.

Sterling looked at Sara. "How about it?"

"Um. What is it?"

He smiled. "It's an Italian cocktail with equal parts gin, sweet vermouth, and Campari."

"Garnished with orange peel," the server added helpfully. "I peeled them this morning."

"Sounds good...if you'll have one?"

Sterling nodded. "I will have a small one."

"They're all one size," the server said quickly.

"Yes, it was just a joke. Not a very good one, I'm afraid." Sterling smiled patiently. "Can we have it while we wait for the food, please, and we'll order now." He glanced at Sara. "Shall I just pick something?"

"Yes, please," she said, grateful not to have to decide. "I think the place must be under new management. They only used to have hot dogs and burgers."

"Yes, it changed hands a couple of weeks ago," Sterling said. "We'll have the queen's ocean seafood platter please, as well as the grilled mahi-mahi."

The kid left with the orders, and Sara leaned back in the comfortable chair. Suddenly, she couldn't think of another thing to say. But it didn't matter, because after a brief moment of gazing out at the sea, her boss began to talk about cases from the past, the books he read at home, about playing the piano, about the water, the sea, and the sky.

Their conversation flowed easy; there was always something else to mention, something new to make Sara smile.

The Negroni arrived, and they sipped it while looking out at the gorgeous blue sea. "Oops." Sara giggled when she set down her empty glass. "I think I'm thirsty. I didn't mean to drink so fast."

"I feel the same." Sterling turned to catch the server's eye, and he soon came to check on them. "Can we get the Tropical Fruit Sangria and the Coconut Mojito? Also sparkling water, please, and the coconut shrimp for an appetizer."

The drinks and appetizer came quickly, and Sterling let Sara choose her drink. She picked the coconut mojito. Leaning back in her chair, her eyes on the sunny sea and cold cocktail in hand, Sara felt like she was having the most luxurious spa day.

"This is nice." Smiling, she shaded her eyes and glanced at her boss.

"I'm glad." Sterling had taken off his suit jacket and now rolled up his shirt sleeves, smiling back at her. "I've been meaning to ask you for a while—how are you, Sara?"

CHAPTER 27

I 'm very good indeed." Sara took another sip from the pink straw, wondering why he was asking and immediately forgetting because her coconut mojito was delicious. It was a sumptuous blend of white wine, tropical juices, and fresh fruit slices, served over ice with a splash of sparkling water. "I've never had one of these either. It's delicious and refreshing!" she reported, flashing her boss a wide smile.

She remembered smiling like this when she was young. It used to be her trademark; people always commented on her smile. But that was a long time ago, so long, she'd forgotten about it until now.

Sterling nodded. "Try the grilled shrimp; they're good. And the mango dipping sauce is freshly made." He pushed the plate closer to her. "Excuse me for one moment." He stood and went inside.

Sara tried the appetizer. The shrimp were coated in a crispy coconut crust, lightly fried, and grilled to golden perfection. Sterling returned before long with a new story about an old client, and they talked, helping themselves to delicious bites in between sips of cocktail.

They were just splitting the last two shrimp when an enormous seafood platter arrived. They each helped themselves to crab claws, oysters on the half shell, lobster meat, and mussels, and then Sterling cheered Sara with an oyster. "Bon appétit."

Smiling, she touched his shell with one of her own, and then they ate. There was more than enough, and the grilled mahi-mahi arrived before the platter was half-empty. The fish was grilled to perfection and simply melted in Sara's mouth. Regretfully, she eyed the sides. But she was simply too full to eat the cilantro-lime rice or to do more than nibble on the warm corn tortillas filled with avocado slices, Pico de Gallo, and creamy chipotle sauce.

Unable to take another bite, Sara was dabbing her mouth with the napkin when she caught Sterling's eye. He was leaning back, his arms crossed, smiling at her.

"When did you finish eating?" Sara let her napkin sink, smiling back at him guiltily. "I could've sworn you were right there with me."

"Oh, I am. I was." His throat moved with an inner dialog before he spoke. "I've wanted to do this for a very long time," he said.

There was something new in his voice, something that Sara hadn't heard before. Slowly, she tipped her head. What exactly did he mean? "You did?"

"Yes." He leaned back, the tone of his voice normal again. "I meant to go to the bistro so many times, but whenever I finally made my way down here, it was closed."

"I'm sorry." Sara wasn't sure what she was sorry about. That the bistro was often closed, that she'd eaten so much, or maybe that Sterling's voice was back to normal?

"Not at all. Erm, Sara—I hate to say this, but..."

"Yes." She sat up straight. Had they exceeded his budget? She was prepared to shoulder her half of the bill. The meal had been fantastic, the best she'd had in years, something out of a fantasy. So worth it. She'd just skimp on coffee and lunches for the next month. She could make sandwiches at home and bring her coffee from—

"Dessert." Sterling raised an eyebrow. "It's very important."

"Oh!" Surprised, she chuckled. "No, really, Mr. Sterling, let's not order more. I can't eat another bite."

"Of course you don't have to eat anything if you don't want to." From the corner of her eye, Sara saw the server approach with a full tray. "But the tiramisu looked so tempting when I went inside to pay, I'm afraid I ordered already."

Sara cleared her throat. Somehow, he'd read her thoughts about splitting the bill. "Are you sure?" she said quietly. "It's a lot."

His patient smile told her that he knew this wasn't about the tiramisu. "Sara, it's nothing. It's lunch. I'm just glad you were able to make time."

Their server set two plates with creamy tiramisu on the table, and another server arrived with a coffee in a tall glass and a steaming espresso cup that Sterling claimed for himself.

"What's this?" Sara took the tall glass the server handed her.

"Iced caramel macchiato," he said. "Anything else?"

"No, that's it. Thanks very much." Sterling nodded.

Sara tried her drink. It was a smooth espresso blended with creamy milk and sweet caramel syrup, served over ice and topped with a swirl of whipped cream.

"Is it good?" Sterling asked.

"It is heaven." Sara wouldn't have thought of ordering an iced coffee on top of the delicious meal, but it was decadent perfection. "How is your espresso?"

He took a sip and nodded thoughtfully. "Maybe a darker roast would be better. But it's pretty good."

"Pretty good." She shook her head and took another long drink, and then she picked up her spoon. At this point, it didn't matter anymore. "All right." She nodded at him. "I'm past good and evil. I'll just eat everything now. If you don't have your dessert now, I'm probably going to eat that too."

"Ah, no, I think I'll have it myself. But I'm glad you're enjoying yourself, Sara. You work too much."

"Oh, look who's talking." She put a forkful of the tiramisu in her mouth. Layers of delicate mascarpone cream, espresso-soaked ladyfingers, and a hint of cocoa melted on her tongue, culminating in a blissful burst of sweetness and the subtle bitterness of coffee. She sighed happily. "So beautiful."

Sterling smiled. "Very beautiful."

The tone of his voice...

Slowly, Sara set her fork down. Suddenly, she couldn't eat another bite or take another sip. She almost couldn't breathe. And she couldn't pretend she didn't know exactly what he meant.

"Julian..." she said softly, knowing she didn't need to say more.

"Yes," he replied after a brief moment. "Yes, I know."

"I'm..." She didn't know what to say. Her head was empty, as if the tide had swept all her thoughts and feelings and sensations into the sea.

He pushed his chair back. "Well. Should we go back, Sara? I've claimed your company long enough. It's getting late, and your family will want you back."

"Yes," she whispered and set her napkin on the table. "Let's go back, Julian."

CHAPTER 28

"Hannah?"

When she heard the nurse call, Hannah looked up from her book. She'd been catching up on her chapters for the book club while Tommy was sleeping peacefully, his eyes closed and his tiny chest rising and sinking regularly.

The nurse waved Evan into the room. He looked disheveled, as if he'd slept in his car for days. "Hannah?" He shuffled closer, nervously adjusting his visitor badge. "Hey, Hannah."

"Hey. Come here, Evan." Hannah slipped her book into her bag and pulled the strap over her shoulder.

The nurse left, and Evan came to the incubator. His eyes were wide open as he took in his newborn son. "Is this him?" he asked, awe in his voice.

"Yes." Hannah smiled. "He's a beautiful baby. Congratulations, Dad."

Evan gave her an awkward smile caught between shame and pride. "I didn't know it would be today. I can't believe I missed it."

Hannah nodded. "I suppose that's what happens when you build a life on lies. You miss out on the good things. The ones life is all about."

Slowly, Evan returned his gaze to his son. "Did she tell you his name? Last time she and I talked, we hadn't settled yet, and she was too upset to tell me when she called. She barely told me the hospital."

Hannah clicked her tongue, the sound full of pity. Evan had wanted to be a dad so bad, and then he missed the birth of his son because of his lies. "His name is Tommy. He's going to be okay. His lungs are catching up."

"Tommy. Thomas." Evan put a hand on the incubator and, for a long while, gazed at the newborn. Then he quietly cleared his throat. "Did you talk to her, Hannah?"

"Alli? Yes. I was with her when her water broke, and I was outside her room when she gave birth. She asked me to stay with her. At least she wasn't alone, Evan."

"That's good." He swallowed, his throat moving. "Thank you, Hannah. I didn't know you were still in Mendocino Beach."

"Alli spent the last few days in some shady sublet situation, Evan." Gathering her purse and farmers market bag with the stale rolls, Hannah rose to leave. "Make sure she has a place to go. Make sure she'll be close to her family and friends. She'll need them."

"I will. I brought a car seat for the baby. I brought... I will take care of them." His voice was hoarse. "Hannah?"

"What?" She turned to look over her shoulder.

"For what it's worth—I'm sorry for what I did to you. You deserved better, and I knew it all along."

"Why didn't you just tell me? You could have broken it off." She looked at her hands. "I'd have let you go, Evan."

He took a short, gasping breath, quiet and low, as if he were choking. "I didn't want to let you go," he murmured. "I couldn't. After all you went through with..." He stopped talking and glanced at the baby.

"Well." Hannah smiled sadly. "You made it worse."

For a moment, he closed his eyes. Then he said, "I know I'm only here because you talked Alli into letting me come. I'm grateful, Hannah."

She looked at him, really taking in the image of the man who had once, more than four years ago, been her husband. "I'm getting a lawyer, Evan," she said softly and pulled her purse strap over her shoulder. "Take good care of your son. Respect Alli's wishes. You owe her big."

"I know." He ran a nervous hand through his hair. "I will."

The door opened again, and the nurse, looking slightly harried, poked her head in. "Hannah? An Alexander Shaw is here to take you home?"

Evan's gaze wavered only for a fraction of a moment, but Hannah saw the shock flick across his face.

She nodded at the nurse. "I'm coming. Thank you."

"Who is Alex?" Evan bit his lip.

"He's a friend."

"What sort of friend, Hannah? I've never heard his name."

Hannah walked to the door. She didn't envy Alli the challenges ahead of her. "You don't need to know about my life or the people in it. We are no longer friends, Evan."

"You hate me." She turned and saw the pain in his eyes, the sadness, the longing. He missed her. Despite everything he'd done and all the choices he'd made with his eyes wide open, he missed her. Or at least, the comfort she'd provided in his life.

Her hand on the door handle, Hannah stepped out of the nursery. She felt wonder that she'd stuck with him so long and mild disbelief that he still had no good grasp of his situation. "I don't hate you; I don't have big feelings left for you. I just don't like you."

"That was fast," he murmured.

But she had caught the quiet words. "Not really. I think I haven't liked you in a long time." She tipped her head, thinking. "About four years? Yes. About that long." She raised an eyebrow. "Does that make sense to you, Evan?"

Again, his throat moved with unspoken words and suppressed feelings. "Yes," he finally murmured. "That makes sense, Hannah. I'm sorry."

Careful not to startle the newborns, she softly closed the door and left.

Alex was sitting on a club chair in the lobby downstairs, drumming his fingers on the armrest. He was wearing his eye patch and had a brooding, grumpy expression on his face.

And yet—as soon as Hannah saw him, everything else faded away. The pity, the disappointment, the chaos of Tommy's birth. It all melted into the background as she took a deep breath and walked toward Alex, her heart beating lighter with every step.

His blue gaze met hers, and the lines on his face smoothed. He jumped up and came to meet her. "Hannah!"

"Hi, Alex." For a moment, they stood there, looking at each other.

Without thinking, Hannah reached out and took his hand in hers. When his fingers closed around hers, warm and firm and sure, a fire ignited inside her, rising from embers of flames she thought had died long ago.

But here it was, burning bright and strong.

"Are you all right, Hannah?" A line formed between his eyes, and instinctively, he pulled her closer. "I'm so sorry you had to go through this. Are you tired?"

"I'm fine now." Hannah's entire body relaxed toward him. "The nurse said you were here to pick me up. Is that true? It's not your eye, is it?"

"The eye is fine." A smile tugged on the corner of his lips. "Beth told me that you didn't have a ride home." He let go of her hand to reach for the farmers market bag on her shoulder. "Here, let me take that. You've carried enough today." He held out a hand for her bag, and she gave it to him.

"Maybe I did. Thanks." A heartfelt sigh of relief escaped her as she handed over the rolls they'd been supposed to eat for breakfast, and they both had to chuckle at the sound.

"All right." Smiling, he pointed at the exit, and they started walking. "I'm going to take you out to dinner. Let's get some proper food in you before we drive back home."

Her heart warmed at how casually he called his place their home. She wasn't alone. In fact, she was far less alone now than she'd been in her marriage.

She stopped to look at him. "Hey, Alex? Thank you."

"Thank you for what, Hannah?"

She smiled. "Everything. Letting me stay in your place when I had nowhere to go. Putting me in touch with new friends. Coming to get me when I don't have a ride." She reached up and cradled his cheek in her hand, letting her thumb run over the stubble. "Thank you for being a good person, Alex. Thank you for caring."

"I do care." He caught her hand. "But I think we should talk, Hannah."

Her heart hiccupped. The last time a man told her they had to talk, it didn't go well. But this man was not like the other. And this time around, she wasn't going to pretend there was nothing to talk about. Bravely, Hannah nodded. "Okay."

He smiled, and when they started walking again, he kept her hand in his.

Outside, night was about to fall. The last streaks of rosy gold and fiery bronze streaked the sky, and the cooling air was fragrant with the resin of pines and sequoias, the sweetness of night-blooming jasmine, and the clean, crisp scent of water babbling a creek nearby in the forest.

When they reached Alex's car, he opened the car door for her.

Hannah was about to sit when she looked at him. His face was only inches from hers. He smelled of black coffee and new books and something else too, something that made it impossible not to lean in for more. Fighting the urge, she smiled. "You're driving with your eye patch?"

His good eye looked back at her, the iris piercing blue even in the dimming light of the summer night. "A lot of people drive wearing their eye patches."

"Hmm. Are you sure your eye is okay?" She squinted, trying to spot a reason why he insisted on wearing it.

"Yes."

She smiled. "Really?"

"Yes."

Slowly, she reached up and lifted the black piece of fabric, just enough to see his star-eye looking back at her. It was just as blue and clear as the other one. "Why are you back to wearing the eye patch, Alex?" she whispered.

Alex squinted over her head at the sky above. "Sometimes, there's nothing worth looking at." His voice was low and deep, coming from a place inside him that only he had seen. But then he lowered his gaze again, meeting hers. "I was worried when you didn't come back from the farmers market. I missed you, Hannah. You were gone all day."

"I missed you too, Alex. I'm glad you came to get me." She reached up and gently threaded the eye patch off his head. "I may no longer be pretty. But...I want to see you. Starry scars and all."

"Not as much as I want to see you." He made a sound that was somewhere between a growl and a threat, and his blue irises flared into icy flames. "Did your husband put that in your head about not being pretty? Did he say you are anything but beautiful?"

Hannah didn't reply. She didn't want Alex to know how ugly she had felt in the last four years. How it felt to have a husband who never complimented her, who slept in another room, who couldn't get himself to mention her looks at all. Maybe she was over Evan. But some wounds, the ones that had already festered for years especially, would take long to scab over and heal.

"He's an idiot and a fool, Hannah," Alex murmured. The car door was between them, but now he reached out and tucked a stray curl behind her ear. "You aren't just pretty." His fingers lingered on the sensitive spot by her ear, trailing along her jaw, making her heart jump in her chest. "You are beautiful. You are more beautiful every time I look at you."

A car door slammed shut near them, and a young man laughed. "Get a room, you two!" he called out good-humoredly as he hurried toward the hospital, a giant bouquet of red roses in his arms.

A crooked smile lifted Alex's lip. "Don't mind if I do," he murmured, just loud enough for Hannah to catch the words. She blushed warmly, and Alex chuckled and stepped back, giving her space to breathe. "Let's go have dinner," he said. "There's a place I want to show you."

CHAPTER 29

They drove through the last of the dying light, brushing along the coast before turning away from the sea and driving uphill.

Hannah, her elbow in the open window and a mild breeze ruffling her curls, didn't ask where they were going. She didn't question their destination; she trusted Alex to take care of her, her mind still lingering on the way he had looked at her in the parking lot.

Soon, their car pulled into a small parking lot, tires crunching on gravel as they parked.

Hannah smiled. "It's a vineyard! What a view!" She had been to other vineyards in the area, but none as charming as this one. The last light was fading into the lavender-blue of a velvety night, casting a soft glow over the sweeping hills and valleys that spread before them. Row after row of vines covered the land, their branches carrying luxurious clusters of red, purple, and green grapes.

"Their wine is great, but the food is even better," Alex promised. "Come on, gorgeous. Let's see what they have for us."

They got out of the car, and Hannah, still tingling from being called gorgeous, deeply inhaled the warm, fragrant evening air. The aroma of sun-ripened grapes mingled with the delicious smells of a charcoal grill, and she suddenly realized how hungry she really was. When the breeze carried the aroma of rosemary and thyme, garlic and sun-dried tomatoes sizzling in olive oil to them, Hannah's stomach growled. She laughed. "Oops."

"Don't worry." Alex smiled at her. "Same." They started walking toward the vinery's roofed terrace. A band at the far end was playing jazz music, and many of the tables were already taken, the soft chatting and laughter of the vineyard guests as welcoming as the view and the fragrant air.

A party of four was just leaving, and a young server seated Hannah and Alex at their table by the railing. "Couldn't have picked a better spot," Hannah said gratefully.

The day had been jam-packed with mixed emotions and complicated feelings, old conflict and new resolution. But now that she was here, with Alex, she felt safe, comfortable, and happy.

"Good evening." A new server brought menus, and her face lit up with recognition. "You are Hannah! Aren't you?"

Hannah looked up. She'd seen the young woman before, and it didn't take long for the penny to drop. "Zoe! From the restaurant in Mendocino Cove!"

"Yes, the Mermaid Galley." Smiling, Zoe pulled out a notepad and pencil. "I work here too. I'm trying to scrape together the money to buy a bakery."

"I'll be your first customer." Hannah beamed.

Zoe nodded. "I always wondered how you were doing."

"Much better than when we last met." Impulsively, Hannah stood and pulled Zoe into a hug. "You were the first one to give me a hand when I needed it most. I'll never forget it."

"Nah, no worries." Flushing with pleasure, Zoe hugged Hannah back before letting her go. "I'm glad to see you again. So, what can I get you?"

"Wine?" Alex smiled at Hannah. "I think you deserve a glass of something good. Maybe we can get a recommendation?"

"Yes, please. Wine sounds great."

"I'll bring you something nice to go with dinner." Zoe thoughtfully tapped her pencil against her lower lip. "I highly recommend the ribeye steak and the grilled halibut with a creamy herb and citrus sauce. The kitchen has outdone themselves with those tonight."

Alex slid his menu back with a satisfied look. "Steak works for me."

"And I'd love the halibut, actually." Hannah handed her menu back as well. "You had me at cream sauce."

A man in his fifties, with tan skin, silver hair at the temples, and laughing eyes, stopped on his way past the table. "Did I hear someone order the halibut?"

"And steak." Zoe smiled. "This is Jon Donovan, the owner of the vineyard," she introduced him. "Jon, these are Hannah, of Mendocino Beach, and...um..." She looked expectantly at Alex.

"Alex Shaw," Hannah repaid the favor of introduction. "He owns the bookstore in Mendocino Beach."

"Really!" Jon held out a hand. "I remember the last owner; he was a friend of my dad's." His lips curved into a smile. "If I remember right, you look an awful lot like him."

"He was my dad." Alex stood and shook Jon's hand. "Nice to meet you, Jon."

"Good to meet you too. I heard something about his son being in the military, is that right? I'm glad you found your way back home. We should catch up sometime soon. The vinery's doors are always open for old friends."

"Ex-military. Would be my pleasure."

Jon smiled at Hannah. "Do you enjoy Mendocino?"

"I love it," she replied sincerely. "I grew up in Mendocino Beach and just returned to live here. I'm hoping to get our old family home back."

"Ah. Best of luck. My wife, Jenny, also returned here not too long ago." The look in his eyes softened when he said her name, but then he smiled. "Let's get you settled for dinner. For the steak, I'd say the cabernet sauvignon. It has notes of dark berries and cedar. Works well with grilled meat."

"Sounds great." Alex nodded and sat back down.

"And for the grilled halibut..." Jon turned to Hannah. "I've got a very nice sauvignon blanc. It's crisp, with light citrus flavors. The perfect match for the halibut."

"Sounds lovely." Hannah smiled back. She was getting used to having people in the know decide what would be the most delicious food and drink for her, and she liked it very much indeed.

"I'll get to it. Enjoy." Jon knocked on the table and left. Zoe picked up the menus. "Be right back with a breadbasket." She left, returning her notepad to the pocket of her black half-apron.

The jazz music slowed into a new melody. Several couples rose to dance in the center space of the terrace, while others stayed seated, eating and laughing with friends and family.

"I love the fireflies," Hannah said dreamily, propping her chin in her hand and looking out at the rolling hills. "Look, Alex." She pointed at the rows of vines. The last light of the sun had vanished, replaced with the twinkle of string lights under the roof and the silver glow of a waxing moon.

In the grapevines, the dry yellow grass, the branches of the old oaks, and the shadows sparkled and flashed the lights of thousands, if not millions, of fireflies. "Isn't that pretty?"

"Beautiful." Alex smiled, but his gaze was on Hannah, not the sparkling hills.

When she noticed it, she smiled back, butterflies stirring in her stomach. "No, really, Alex. Look."

"I *am* looking. I thought I'd seen enough when I came back from the war, so I kept wearing the eye patch. But I don't need it anymore, not now that you are home. I want to see you with both eyes, Hannah." He stood and extended his hand toward her. "I can't remember the last time I danced. Will you do me the honor?"

The invitation startled her. Hannah couldn't remember the last time she had danced either. Evan had never... She blinked, stopping herself as she rose.

It no longer mattered what her ex had or had not done. Hannah's past had no hold over her here, in this beautiful night, in the company of this man.

Smiling, her heart beating a little faster, she gave Alex her hand. "I'd love to dance with you, Alex Shaw," she said softly, marveling at how alive, happy, and safe she felt with him.

He led her to the dance floor and gently took her into his arms. Protected by the strength of his embrace, Hannah relaxed completely. Not caring what anyone thought, she closed her eyes and rested her cheek against his shoulder.

"You smell of roses," he murmured, his arms tightening as he guided her steps to the music. "The yellow roses that grow at the bookstore."

"And you smell of books and coffee." She smiled softly. "I didn't know you could dance."

Something brushed her hair. His chin—or his lips? "There's a lot you don't know about me, Hannah."

She lifted her head to look into his blue, starry eyes. "There's also a lot you don't know about me, Alex."

He tightened his arms even more, pulling her closer. She again rested her head on his shoulder. "I hate that you are married," he whispered, his voice so low she could barely hear it.

"Only in name. Everything else—it's all over. I'm divorcing him. Or maybe he's divorcing me. It doesn't matter anymore."

"Are you going to let him have your house?"

"Why?" She smiled.

"Because it's yours. Because you belong in Mendocino Beach. Unless you want to leave again?"

"No," she whispered. "I want to live here. I've always wanted to live here."

"Really?" He stopped and gently lifted her chin with his finger. "Do you mean that?" His gaze held hers captive. "Tell me what you really think, Hannah. I don't play. That's one thing you don't yet know about me."

She reached up, burying her hands in his hair. It was soft and full despite its short length, and she ran a finger along the silver strand at his temple, smiling at his earnest face. "I know you've been hurt before. But just so you know—as far as I'm concerned, I'm no longer married and I'm staying in Mendocino Beach. Do what you think is right, Alex."

Another song ended, and the music faded. The surrounding guests erupted into applause, the jazz musicians acknowledging the break with quick sips from their wine glasses. And yet, in that moment, it felt as though Hannah and Alex were the only two people in the moonlight on the terrace.

"If that is really how you feel..." His chest heaved with a deep, steadying breath. He gently cupped her face, his thumb brushing against her cheek. "But I know how hard it can be to let go of the past. A divorce is one thing. But opening your heart to love again? That's another thing, Hannah." His eyes searched her face. "With you, I don't want just a taste and a trial. I don't want half-hearted."

"What do you want?" she whispered.

"I want it all. Are you ready to give love a second chance?"

CHAPTER 30

Hannah was no longer bound, and she knew she was falling fast and hard for Alex Shaw. But was it too early to love again? Was she truly fully ready to give her heart—not just bits and pieces but all of it, the whole entire thing—to a man?

"I don't know, Alex," Hannah whispered, holding his gaze as the musician started a new tune. "I can't tell."

Alex lowered his head slightly toward her, his eyes on her lips. "But you have thought about it?" he asked in a rough whisper. "Tell me the truth."

"Yes, I have." Hannah was not afraid of this conversation. It was okay to let him know how she truly felt, to be honest about how flawed she was, how vulnerable, how unsure. Alex wouldn't run away from a conversation. "My life has been a whirlwind ever since I arrived in Mendocino Beach," Hannah admitted. "I want to be with you. But how can I tell if I'm truly ready to love?" A frown lowered her brows. "I don't want to mess this up. I don't want to hurt you. I don't want you to hurt ever again, Alex."

"Hmm." Slowly, he straightened his back, and then he took her hand and led her from the dance floor to the terrace's balustrade, where it was quiet and dark but for the moonlight and the soft glow of string lights. "It makes a lot of sense, Hannah. I understand what you're saying." He put a hand on the balustrade, shielding her from the cooling breeze that rustled the vines. "For what it's worth...I am ready." He looked at her, his starry eye silver in the night. "I am ready, Hannah," he repeated in a voice that made her heart do a double take.

"How do you know you are truly ready?" she asked.

"I know. I've been waiting for you. Even when I was married, I was waiting for you; I understand that now. I didn't back then." He shook his head at the memory of his former self. "Believe me, I was trying my hardest to love her wholeheartedly. I thought something was wrong with me, that I had commitment issues and needed to twist myself into someone I wasn't. But now I know what it was." He took a breath. "I realized it when I looked up and there you were, standing in my bookstore." He reached up and let a curl glide through his hand. "Curls and eyes and heart and all," he murmured.

"Oh, why can I not remember you?" Hannah didn't know whether to laugh or cry. "Remind me, Alex! Did we do a lot of things together?"

"Ah." He gently touched the tip of her nose with his finger. "Not as much as I'd have liked, but I did what I could. I walked you home from school. Got you out of more than one tight spot at recess too, Hannah Banana. I'll show you the journal I kept sometime. You'll remember." He shook his head, amused. "You always told me about the books you were reading with your mom."

A soft laugh escaped her. "I remember talking about books nonstop. It was my escape."

"I know. And you were always so passionate about it. That's one of the things I loved about you, even back then." His smile faded into a tender expression. "I never forgot you, Hannah. Those memories kept me going more times than you could imagine."

Her heart swelled with emotion. "I'd love to see that journal, Alex. And maybe we can make some new memories."

He lifted her hand to his lips, pressing a gentle kiss to her knuckles. "I'd like that," he said softly. "Very much."

She tried to steady her breathing. The man was too attractive for his own good—or rather, hers. "But...I came to the bookstore every Saturday!" she said quickly. "I remember all about the store. You weren't there."

"I was with my mother on weekends." He cleared his throat, steadying himself. "Listen, I'd rather you take your time and be sure you know what you want. I'm not going anywhere. And whatever you decide, Hannah—I can handle it. Don't worry about hurting my feelings. We are not too far out at sea yet, and I'm a good sailor." He tucked a curl behind her ear. "Okay?"

"Thank you, Alex," she whispered. Maybe she didn't remember him in images or actions but as a feeling. She remembered once feeling as safe and happy as she did now, with him.

"All right. Let's just have dinner tonight." The crooked smile tugged again at his lips. Hannah didn't think she'd ever get tired of seeing it. He took her hand. "Come on. Our wine just arrived."

Hannah gathered her courage. "Alex? Listen, this all goes both ways, okay? I don't want to lead you on."

"Lead me on?" His eyebrows rose in surprise, and then he chuckled. "You couldn't lead me on if you tried, gorgeous."

Hannah smiled as she followed him through the dancers back to the table. "Oh, no? You sure?"

He grinned at her as they sat, but then his expression turned serious and he leaned across the table so she could hear his low voice. "I don't know how your ex treated you," he said softly. "But you're safe with me. If you've had enough of men and just want peace and quiet, have peace and quiet. You don't have to walk on eggshells with me or tell me what you think I want to hear. But while you do think it over, I will—"

He leaned back as a teenage server slid their steaming dinner plates onto the table.

When the server was gone, Hannah tilted her head. "While I think it over—what will you do?"

"I'll still steer my ship where I want it to go. I'll be the one making sure you have a safe place to stay and good books to read. I'll take you to dinner and be your ride home, and I'll make sure you start your mornings with hot coffee and warm cinnamon rolls." Alex lifted his wine glass. "My plan is to help you with thinking it over."

"Sounds lovely." Touched, and curious if he'd keep those promises, Hannah raised her wine glass too. "I don't deserve you, Alex. You're a good friend."

He lightly clinked his glass against hers but shook his head as if she'd made a mistake. "Wrong on both counts, gorgeous." He took a sip of his wine.

"Oh." Hannah drank too. Her head was swirling with the pace of their conversation. An hour ago, she'd been watching her husband's newborn, telling him to take care of the other woman. And now, Alex was telling her he'd always loved her and asked whether she was ready for a second chance at love. The golden wine was clear and cool, and she let the clean, crisp notes of sun and sweet grapes and citrus roll over her tongue. Twirling the stem between her fingers, she looked up. "All right, handsome. Tell me—how am I wrong?"

"I'm not a friend, and you deserve the best," he said, matter-of-fact. "Let's eat before this gets cold."

The food was so good Hannah found herself pleasantly distracted from the tumult of emotions swirling inside her. Despite the butterflies in her stomach, she savored each bite of the grilled halibut, its tender texture and delicate flakes melting in her mouth with every delicious bite.

"Like it?"

"Very much." She offered him a taste. Without hesitation, he took her fork and tried the fish.

"Mh-mm. Almost as good as the ribeye." He cut off a piece of grilled meat and held it out, raising a seductive eyebrow.

Smiling, she took it. If this was how it would always be, she was ready enough for her second chance at love. Maybe if one's husband had checked out four years ago—five? eight?—the period of grief after divorce really was just extremely short...

"Hmm. It's excellent!" Her eyes widened. The tender ribeye had been marinated in a savory blend of garlic, rosemary, and olive oil and grilled to perfection over an open flame. "Um. How are the roast potatoes?" She grinned.

"Have one and see for yourself." Alex offered her his plate with a gesture to help herself, and she tried the potatoes. They were perfectly seasoned, crispy-brown on the outside and sweet and fluffy on the inside as if they'd been slow-roasted in foil in embers and ashes.

"Wow." Hannah nodded her acknowledgment. "You know, divorce one way or the other... I can't remember the last time I ate as well as I have since coming to Mendocino."

Alex put his fork and knife down.

"What does that look mean?" she asked softly.

"I wonder... Ah." He rubbed his hands over his face.

"What do you wonder?"

"If he didn't even make sure you got to enjoy the pleasure of good food..." He didn't complete the sentence, but his *what else* hung in the air between them, nevertheless. "No wonder you're not sure you want to take another chance at love."

Hannah's heart skipped a beat. This wasn't just about food; she sensed the unspoken question lingering in his gaze. Memories of intimacy with her husband had become a distant echo.

She met Alex's gaze, feeling an embarrassed warmth spreading through her chest. It was a delicate dance, this prospect of rediscovering intimacy after so much hurt. "It wasn't just the food," she admitted, her voice carrying the weight of years spent in emotional isolation. "It's been a while."

Their eyes locked, a silent understanding passing between them. Alex reached across the table, his fingertips grazing hers, sending a shiver down her spine. "I understand," he murmured, his voice gentle yet filled with a silent promise of deeper pleasures in her life than just food and drink.

Hannah's breath caught in her throat as she felt the last walls around her heart begin to crumble. With Alex, it was different. There was a tenderness in his touch, a sincerity in his words, an openness to their communication that made her believe. In true love and soul mates and all the other things she'd put on the heap of discarded dreams.

"Okay?" He sat back, giving her space, his eyes still full of warmth and reassurance.

She nodded, a small smile playing on her lips. Was he aware of just how swiftly he sailed his ship in the direction of his desire? "Okay." She dabbed her lips with her napkin, and then, following an impulse, she pushed back her chair and stood. "Would you like to dance with me, Mr. Shaw?"

"Almost as much as I'd like to do other things with you, Miss Banner," he murmured, his gaze lingering on her in a way that made hot blood rush to her cheeks as if she'd never dated a man before. He rose, wrapping his arm around her waist—strong, reassuring, and full of promise—to lead her back to the dance floor.

"Excuse me, ma'am? Excuse me. Pardon the interruption." A tall, well-groomed man rose from the table behind them. He wore neatly pressed slacks and a white button-up shirt with the sleeves rolled up. His dark hair was impeccably styled, and his eyes held a confident glint as he approached.

CHAPTER 31

Alex stopped without letting go of Hannah. "Can I help you?"

The man inclined his head toward Hannah. "May I have a quick word with you?"

"What's this about?" Alex asked, his grip tightening protectively.

"It's all right, Alex." Hannah patted his arm reassuringly. "I'll just be a moment." She felt safe in this lively setting, surrounded by laughter and music, and the man's silver-templed appearance seemed trustworthy.

Reluctantly, Alex let her go. "I'll check on dessert," he said softly into her hair. "If you need me, just call."

"Will do." Smiling, Hannah gently extricated herself from Alex's arm and gestured toward the private space between the tables and the terrace's balustrade. "What's this about?"

The man followed her to the space, keeping a respectful distance. "I apologize again—I don't usually do this. Here's my card." He produced the promised card from his wallet and handed it to Hannah.

"Julian Sterling, Attorney at Law," she read and looked up. "How can I help you, Mr. Sterling?"

"Well, this is awkward, but I hope you'll forgive me. I was sitting at the table next to yours and couldn't help overhear parts of your conversation."

Hannah felt taken aback. Had the man been eavesdropping on what she considered a very private conversation? "You did?"

"Again, I apologize. I moved to the other side of the table eventually since you seemed..." He cleared his throat. "I didn't mean to intrude. However, I believe my paralegal assistant is a friend of yours. Her name is Sara Reynolds?"

Hannah appreciated that he'd moved further away but still felt a little tight-lipped. "I know Sara. We're in the same book club."

"Right." He nodded, looking completely at ease. "And if I may—in the strictest confidence, Sara once very briefly mentioned a married friend who just bought a house that used to belong to her mother. However, the husband of said friend betrayed her in the most unforgivable way and claimed the house since his name was on the deed."

"Um..." Who else had Sara told Hannah's life story in the strictest confidence?

He smiled. "Sara was quite upset over the unfair treatment of her friend. I can't help but think you might be..."

"Yes." Hannah cleared her throat. "It's me. And she's right. Evan said he paid for the house with the money he earned at his job while I mucked around with books, so the house should be his and I should have the car."

She thought for a moment. "I'm a librarian. But I didn't earn as much as he did, so I suppose he did buy the house with his money."

"No." Sterling smiled politely. "Oh, no. Have you looked into California divorce law at all?"

"I'm getting around to it now because I want my mother's house." Hannah crossed her arms. It was best to be honest. "But I don't have much money for a lawyer, and Evan has already done his legwork. I'm not sure I can catch up."

"I'm an experienced divorce lawyer," Sterling said. "You are Sara's friend, a local, and a librarian." His smile deepened, reaching his cocoa-brown eyes. "I would like to take on your case pro bono. That means, for free."

"For free? As in, you'll waive your fee?" she repeated, dumbfounded. "Really?"

"Absolutely." He pointed at the card. "It'll be my pleasure to get you a divorce and a fair share of joint property." He raised an eyebrow. "Which can include the house, if you want it. Think it over. You know where to find me."

"Wow. Did Sara ask you for this?"

"No, she did not." He smiled. "But would it be so bad if she had?"

"I just..." Hannah inhaled. "Yes. I accept your kind offer. Thank you."

Sterling tipped his head. "You accept?"

She nodded, nervously kneading her fingers. "If you really mean it."

"I really mean it," he assured her. "I really, *really* mean it. I'd much rather the houses in town belong to my—to Sara's friends than their cheating husbands."

Hannah moistened her lips, already nervous at the thought of legal battles. "So...what do we do?"

He smiled. "We meet. Tomorrow, if you can. We'll start by gathering all the necessary information and documentation related to your marriage. I'd like to have all the details about your assets, liabilities, income, expenses, and any relevant agreements or disputes between you and your spouse. Then, we'll work together to develop a strategy and begin the legal process of filing for divorce. I'll advocate for your interests and ensure that your rights are protected every step of the way."

"I'm not sure—" She took a shaky breath, her voice wavering slightly. "Yes. Okay."

He cleared his throat, sounding like he was swallowing laughter. "It's not as scary as it sounds. Do you have access to the paperwork regarding your assets?"

Nervously, Hannah tapped a finger to her chin. Evan had been the one in charge of money matters in their marriage, but... "You know, all our files are in the truck with my books. It's stuck on top of the mountain range. They had to fix something in the engine and are waiting for parts."

"And the name of the moving company?"

"Swift and Safe."

"Ah yes. No worries, I've dealt with them before." Mr. Sterling nodded, looking like he knew exactly how to get that truck down the mountain within the hour. "Can you meet at nine in my office tomorrow? I'm near the harbor." He pulled out his phone to make a note.

"Of course." Gratitude rushed through Hannah. She'd already wondered whether she would have to drive up the mountain and unload the truck carload by carload. If he was as competent with the divorce as he was with the moving company, she had just been given a golden ticket. "I can...uh, can I bring breakfast? Maybe bagels?"

Sterling looked up at her, his expression unreadable. "Bagels would be lovely, Hannah. I like sesame, if it's no bother."

She smiled. "It's no bother."

Smiling back, he inclined his head in farewell. "See you tomorrow, then."

Mr. Sterling had barely left when Alex returned, carrying a round pizza board. "Is he gone?" He looked after Sterling, who was striding quickly toward the parking lot.

"Yes." Hannah took a deep breath. "He is." She returned to her chair and sank into it with a sigh of relief. "Whew."

"Whew, what?" Alex set the tray on their table and sat down as well. "Tell me what's going on over dessert. I got us a Mendocino apple caramel tart with vanilla ice cream. I thought we could share."

"We sure can." The dessert was large enough to feed a family of four. Like an enormous French galette, the thin, flaky crust was covered with cinnamon-sugar-glazed apple slices and drizzled with golden-brown caramel, folded up at the edges. Vanilla ice cream and tufts of whipped cream slowly melted on top of the warm caramel.

"Are you a romantic, Alex?" Hannah smiled as she inhaled the warm aroma of cinnamon sugar, baked apples, vanilla bean, and caramel.

The string lights cast soft shadows on the sharp lines of his face. "Only for the right woman," he said simply. "For her, roses and desserts and dancing in the moonlight are part of the package. Not every woman enjoys that, by the way." He looked up. "What about you, Hannah?"

Touched, Hannah held out her hand across the table, and Alex took it. "I love romance," she said quietly. "I love when a man can show his affection."

His blue gaze dropped to her lips where it lingered before roaming back to her eyes. "What did the man want from you, Hannah?" He let go of her hand and picked up a knife. "He'd better have had a good reason to interrupt us. I don't often get asked to dance, you know."

She leaned back. "He's a lawyer. His name is Julian Sterling."

Alex raised his eyebrows. "That was Julian Sterling? The man himself?"

"Yes. Do you know him?"

"I know of him, though we never met. He's Sara's boss. Apparently, he works for a lot of Hollywood celebrities but chooses to live here and only flies to LA when he can't avoid it. How on earth is Evan able to afford him?" Alex shook his head as he cut into the dessert. "I'm sorry, Hannah. Sterling will rake you over the coals, but we got this." He placed a generous slice of caramel apple pie, topped with vanilla ice cream and whipped cream, onto a plate and handed it to her. "Whatever happens between the two of us—you're welcome to stay over the bookstore for as long as you want."

"Thank you, Alex." Gratitude for his friendship filled her once more as she took the plate. "But I've got good news! Sterling wants to work for me, and he wants to do it pro bono."

Alex looked up, surprised. "For real?"

"At least that's what he said." She pulled the card from her pocket and held it out for Alex to see. "He gave me this."

Alex rubbed a hand over his chin as he studied the classy, embossed card. "Did he say why?"

Hannah thought about their conversation. "Sara told him what Evan did," she finally said. "And I don't think Mr. Sterling likes him much."

Alex nodded, chewing the inner corner of his lips. "He's got a good point right there."

"I also think he likes Sara. Sterling, that is."

"Sara's married."

"I didn't say he likes her like *that*." Though it was possible, now that Hannah remembered the look in Julian Sterling's cocoa eyes, that he did like Sara like that.

"What else?"

She smiled. "He also likes librarians."

"Hmm. How much does he like librarians?"

"Not like *that*." She laughed. "Not like that, Alex."

He grinned. "Good. I was just starting to like the man."

Hannah tried her galette. It tasted of cinnamon sugar and caramel, and the apples were sweet and tender with just the right amount of bite. The vanilla ice and whipped cream perfectly balanced the pie. Taking her time to savor her dessert, she put the last bite in her mouth. "Mh-mm." She sighed contentedly and used her napkin to wipe a speck of ice cream off her fingers. "What a full day and magical night it's been, Alex."

"Are you done?" He had long since finished and was sitting, arms crossed over his chest, watching her.

"Yes. It's a pity, but I simply can't eat another bite." Few people were eating dinner anymore, but everyone was enjoying wine and cheese platters, coffee and apple galettes, and many couples were still dancing.

He rose. "I'm taking you home."

"Oh?" She tilted her head. "You still owe me a dance, Alex. I'm not that tired. Are you?"

"The problem is that the longer I look at you, the less tired I feel." He leaned across the table, wiping a crumb of caramel sugar off her chin. "You're too sweet for your own good, Miss I-still-need-time-to-think. I'm going to take a rain check." He held out this hand. "Come on, gorgeous. Let's go home."

Smiling, Hannah took his hand and stood. Her mind wandered to her quiet room over the bookstore, the soft down pillow on her bed, the quiet song of the sea and cool ocean breeze drifting in through her open window, lulling her to sleep. She yawned, relaxing into the sudden warmth spreading through her body at the thought of slipping into bed.

A soft groan escaped Alex, and he instinctively pulled her to him as they began walking. "I swear you're doing this on purpose," he muttered. "You even smell like caramel and cream."

Unable to resist the urge to be closer to him, she slipped her hand out of his and wrapped her arm around his waist. "I like you, Alex," she murmured sleepily, softly leaning into him and unabashedly reveling in his warmth and strength when he put his arm around her shoulders. "I like you a lot."

CHAPTER 32

"W hat did the game trail camera record?" Sara closed the mystery novel with a frown. "What happened on the field at night? What?"

Hannah laughed. "It doesn't matter."

"It doesn't matter?" Beth slipped her feet out of her loafers and pulled them up on the cozy armchair, picking up her glass of Pinot Grigio. "Why not?"

The soft dark of a new Mendocino summer night had fallen, and the book club had cozied up in the closed bookstore with blankets, snacks, a bottle of red and a bottle of white.

"Because! Don't you see? If the detective had—huh!" One of the candles scattered around the store flickered in its storm glass, and Hannah glanced at it to make sure the flame was safely contained. She did not want Alex to return to the smoking ruin of his store.

Alex had left Mendocino Beach the morning after their dinner at the vineyard. He'd dropped her off at the bottom of the stairs, waiting until she blew a kiss from the landing and went inside.

When she'd stepped back out the next morning, she found a thermos full of piping hot coffee waiting for her, two warm cinnamon rolls in a paper bag from the farmers market, a yellow rose, and a note saying an old friend was experiencing an emergency, and Alex had needed to leave to help out.

Firmly squelching the sinking feeling of disappointment, Hannah ate her breakfast on the top of the stairs, looking out at the ocean and wondering if they'd moved too fast the night before. The tension and desire between them had been heart-poundingly palpable on the ride back home, though he'd not kissed her goodnight.

In the last line of his note, Alex had asked if Hannah could take care of the bookstore while he was gone.

Of course she could. After all he'd done for her, it was the least she could do. Besides, she'd been itching to sort those books properly. So she'd pulled on jeans and a shirt from his closet and marched herself down into the store, where she unlocked the door and perched on Alex's stool behind the counter. Only two people came into the store all day, and none of them bought a book.

How Alex kept the store running, Hannah did not know. Maybe business was really, *really* good around Christmas?

"Hannah? Is Alex still sending you coffee and breakfast every day?" Beth asked softly, calling her back to the present.

She smiled. "Yes, he does. And a good morning text."

Sara studied the charcuterie board on the blanket on the floor and put a slice of prosciutto on a piece of baguette. She bit into it, sighing happily. "He loves you," she announced. "If a man makes sure you have a nice breakfast every day, he's in love. And not only a bit. A lot. Like, madly."

"I don't know." Hannah's cheeks flushed warmly. "We still barely know each other." The texts they exchanged were...not romantic. Normal. Nice. But no burning lover letters.

"You've been through a lot in a short time," Beth pointed out mildly. "He just needs time to take a breather and make sure it's what he really wants."

"Of course." Hannah sipped her Pinot. "It's not like we're attached at the hip, obviously. I'm not keeping track—yet."

Sara finished her snack and wiped her hands on a paper napkin with a pattern of little books. "You know, he does that sometimes. He takes off for a few days, paying someone to keep the store open."

Hannah looked up. "Really?"

Sara picked up another slice of the crusty baguette and spread fig jam on it, topping it off with a slice of cheese. "I only just remembered this morning," she defended herself between bites. "I don't keep track of the man either, you know. I just thought he went fishing or something."

"More likely he is staying away so he doesn't mess things up for you, Hannah. The poor man is only human, if you know what I mean. And if Evan finds out you have an affair before you're divorced, it might play in his favor. By the way." Beth looked between Hannah

and Sara, closing the mystery novel they'd just finished. "Is Sterling making progress?"

"Evan has received the papers." Forgoing sipping,
Hannah drained her glass and set it down, then
dropped her head on the back of her neck and closed
her eyes. She was sitting on a pillow on the floor, her
back propped against the counter, a blanket draped
over her knees. "There's no going back."

"Obviously not," Sara said, sounding satisfied. "By
the way, talk on the street is that he's been making
the rounds, trying to find a lawyer. But nobody wants
to take on Julian."

Hannah blinked an eye open. "I keep trying to put
together how it happened, you know. The things I
did and things he said—it's like I need to inspect
everything in hindsight."

"Sounds like a trauma response. It'll go away eventually. More wine?" Beth asked, sympathy in her
voice.

Hannah shook her head. "No, thank you. I'd better
keep a clear head with all these candles around." The
soft glow of their flames and the silver moonlight
streaming through the windows cozily lit up the store.
But while books, candles, and wine were a match
made in heaven, her job was to safeguard the books.

"So all you need is Evan's signature?" Sara asked.
"What about the house? I'm sure Julian wants you to
have the house."

Just when Hannah was about to answer, there was a
knock on the store's locked front door. They looked

at each other. "Who's that?" Sara let her third piece of baguette with pâté and fig jam sink. "At this hour?"

Beth checked the slim gold watch on her wrist and slipped her feet back into her loafers. "Must be Alex," she said, a little too brightly. "Maybe he lost his key." She got up and went to the door to check.

"Maybe he gave Hannah the only key," Sara said. "The key to *his heart*!"

"Oh...stop it." Smiling, Hannah pushed her blanket back and stood. Her heart was beating faster, and she couldn't help but hope that it was Alex. Despite her meetings with Sterling, despite checking in with Alli and Tommy in the hospital, despite lunches with Sara, dinners with Beth, sunny walks at the beach, and happy afternoons spent sorting books, her week had felt empty. No, not empty—lacking. She missed Alex.

Without him, Mendocino Beach simply wasn't the same.

"Uh. Hannah?" Beth called from the door. "It's Evan."

The anticipation in Hannah's chest curled up its wings and dropped in a deadfall on top of her stomach, pressing on it with a sinking feeling. Hannah hadn't seen or talked to her husband since the day of Tommy's birth.

And she didn't particularly want to see him now, either. Sterling had advised her not to talk to him for the time being.

"Can I come in? Hannah? Can I please have a word?" Evan now called out from the crack in the door.

"Don't!" Sara hissed. "Tell him to speak with Julian!"

"Hannah? Please?"

Hannah heaved a sigh. All those years together—they still counted for something. At least in her book. "Beth, it's okay. I'll talk to him."

"But we're not leaving!" Sara whispered again, a steep line forming between her eyes. "We're staying with you!"

"Thanks." Hannah watched her husband step into the dim store, looking around as if there was something dangerous about the warm, flickering candlelight, the moon shimmer pooling on the old wood floor, the rows of books, and myriad stories surrounding their picnic.

"What are you guys doing here?" His smile was as fake as his voice was nervous.

"Book club." Sara crossed her arms. "Why are you here? The store is closed."

He frowned. "Who are you?"

Sara raised an eyebrow, ready for battle, when Hannah interrupted. "What do you want, Evan?"

He looked at her, and the expression in his eyes became subdued. "Can we talk, Hannah?"

"About what?" There was nothing they needed to talk about. It was all clear, brightly illuminated. What he'd done, what would happen next.

"In private?" He smiled a smile she used to adore. An eternity ago, she would have done anything for a glimpse. Now, it had lost every last speck of magic.

Hannah shook her head. "My friends can hear what you have to say."

A shadow flew over his face and his throat moved as if he wanted to say something, but then he only cleared his throat. "You know, the divorce... I was hoping we could talk about it."

CHAPTER 33

Hannah tipped her head to the side. "What's there to talk about?"

"We need to talk about...all of it."

"I don't understand."

"Erm." He glanced at Sara and Beth, who were watching him with a mix of curiosity and pity, and a breath lifted his chest. "It's just...I finally understand what I've done. How much I messed up."

"You do?" Hannah folded her hands.

"Yes. Yes. I know I was being stupid and...selfish. But, Hannah—I have changed. I want a second chance." His eyelids fluttered.

"A second chance with *me*?" Her eyebrows rose in surprise. "Or with Alli?"

"I know I messed up. I'm... Allison doesn't need me. She doesn't want me." He looked pleadingly at Hannah. "I'm different now. I just want things to go back to the way they used to be."

"You do?" Hannah was almost too stunned to speak. At her side, she could feel Sara's sizzling outrage and Beth's quiet perplexity.

"I'll make it up to you." Evan sounded relieved, as if they'd already agreed to get back together. "You deserve it. I see that now."

Hannah leaned against the counter. "We can't go back to what we had, Evan," she said softly. "You cheated on me for years. You planned a family with another woman. I trusted you. I often felt lonely and ignored in our marriage, but I still trusted you. You hurt me deeply."

His lips moved, and a frown of misery came over his face. But still, he didn't say he was sorry. He didn't care about her loneliness, and her pain, and the fact that he had betrayed her. "Doesn't everyone get a second chance?"

"You already had a second chance," Hannah said after a brief silence. "I gave you a second, and a third, and a fourth chance. You had four years of chances to tell me the truth, to care for my feelings, to respect me. I have no more chances to give you, Evan."

He looked down at his feet before he squared his shoulders. "I'd like you to call off your lawyer, Hannah."

"My lawyer?"

"He wants...too much."

"He says I'm entitled to it by law."

"I've already lost so much when I lost you. And now I lost Alli too. She wants nothing to do with me. I worked hard for the house while you—"

"Muck around with books." Hannah nodded. "You're right, I do. But I'm not stupid. People who muck around with books rarely are. So if my lawyer asks for my fair share, that's fine by me."

"But..." He looked around the room, desperate for a comeback.

"What are you going to do, Evan?" she asked, genuinely curious.

"What can I do?" He met her eyes, and suddenly he looked furious. "I was going to raise my family here! Now I have to hope that I can get my job in San Jose back. Most of my money will go to you and Alli. I won't be able to afford a nice house by the sea. I'll be spending my days at work and my evenings watching TV in a miserable hole! Thanks a lot!"

"I only want my house, Evan," Hannah said firmly. "The house I grew up in, the house my mother loves. You deliberately planned to cheat me out of the house."

"Only the house? No money?" Evan simmered down, clearly conflicted between his anger and the fact that it was less than Sterling demanded.

Hannah nodded. "If you want, you can take the car."

"I get the car? That old thing? It's worth...nothing." His voice faltered as the reversal of his original plan dawned on him.

Hannah chewed her lip. "It's up to you. I'll already get in trouble with my lawyer for offering this much. I'm sure he'd be much happier if I kept the car as well."

Evan ran both his hands through his hair, and then his face crumpled like that of a little boy who'd tripped and spilled his ice cream, and then he reached into the pocket of his jacket and pulled out a key.

"Here." He held it out. "I didn't change anything. Alli never spent a night." He put the key on the counter. "I'll get my things out tonight and put the second key under the mat." He leaned toward her, and Hannah held her breath as his scent enveloped her. She'd never loved how her husband smelled, of new cars and airport lounges, but now it suffocated her.

"Can I have the car key?" he asked. "And a promise that you'll call off your lawyer?"

She nodded. "As soon as you sign the divorce papers."

Wordlessly, Evan pulled out the papers from his back pocket and unfolded them on the counter of the bookstore. "I was hoping to rip this up together with you," he murmured. "Are you sure?"

"I'm sure." She handed Evan a pen, and he signed his name to their divorce.

Feeling a brief pang of pity, a short snap of regret for her past self as a hopeful bride, Hannah went into the backroom to get the car key. If an old car was the price to get Evan out of town, so be it. Everything Hannah needed was right in Mendocino Beach. "Good luck, Evan." A sad smile spread over her lips. "I hope you have a good life."

He took the keys, and for the first time, his lips formed a soundless *sorry*. "You too, Hannah. I know you will. I always want more, but you make the best of what you already have. I'm starting to think that's better." He gave her one last, long look, full of longing for an easier, softer life, and then Evan turned and walked out of the bookstore.

When the door closed shut behind him, Hannah slid down onto the ground, her back against the counter.

"He's gone." Beth went to the door and locked it. "He's gone for good."

Sara picked up the house key from where it lay on the counter and handed it to Hannah. "My boss won't be happy with you," she said mildly. "He was out for a lot more than the house."

"He should take up Alli's case," Hannah said weakly, feeling the weight of the key in her hand. "A single mom needs justice more than I do."

"Now what?" Beth sat back down in her cozy armchair. "Should we go to the house? Make sure he's really getting out?"

Hannah blew out the candle beside her. "Let's go tomorrow. He'll be gone." She felt tired, achy and exhausted, as if she had been in a fistfight. "I'm going to bed."

"Good," Beth said reasonably. "That way, Alex can have this apartment back, though it won't help if his leg doesn't get better. I think he should get a second opinion. Why do men have to be so stubborn when it comes to doctors?"

"The knee isn't injured," Sara said in a low voice. "Alex once mentioned that one of his best friends lost a leg in the same attack Alex's eye was injured. The wound turned septic, and Sam passed away before they could get him out. There was nothing Alex could do to save him. And now his own leg hurts. Same side, too."

Hannah's eyes widened. "I had no idea."

"I've known him a lot longer," Sara said reasonably. "Also, that's just what I think. But I noticed his leg feels better when he's happy."

"You did say he was a good dancer." Beth smiled quietly and started to put the foods back in her basket. "Sounds like his leg works just fine when he takes you out on a date."

"He is an excellent dancer." Hannah rubbed her hands over her face. "Maybe if he can sleep in his bed again, he'll even come back to town."

"It's more likely that it's the signature on your divorce papers that'll do the trick." Sara chuckled and stacked the plates on the empty charcuterie board. "If I were you, I'd text him soon."

Hannah rose to blow out the candles, fold the blanket, and settle the bookstore for the night. "It's Saturday tomorrow. How about we'll start the weekend with mimosas at my house?"

EPILOGUE

Nestled in the rambling garden, overlooking the sparkling sea, and dipped in the glow of the rising morning, Hannah's charming childhood home looked like it had waited for her to return.

The three women climbed onto the sunny front porch. The deck chairs left by the previous owners tempted them to sit and soak in the breathtaking view, but Hannah had to explore first.

"Wow." Sara sounded impressed. "I knew it'd be nice. But this nice? No wonder he wanted it for himself. I want it for *my*self!"

Hannah tore her gaze from the new but familiar sight of the blooming garden and glanced at her friends. With a trembling hand, she lifted the key. "Ready?"

"Hooray!" Sara exclaimed, hoisting the glass bottle of orange juice for mimosas into the air. "Do it!"

"Yes, open the door, Hannah," Beth encouraged, adjusting her grip on the basket of glasses and breakfast foods she carried.

"All right. Here goes." Hannah steadied her arm, inserting the key into the lock and turning it. The door swung open, and she stepped into the house.

It felt like walking into an old dream. The walls, the floors, the rounded doorways, and the wide, cheerful windows—some of them tipped open—were exactly as she remembered. The furniture—the old, comfortable sofa, the dining table, the worn wicker chairs—was all gone. But sunlight flooded the high-ceiling rooms, and it smelled of... She held her nose in the air. "Wait. Does anyone else smell—"

"Cinnamon buns." Sara closed her eyes and inhaled deeply. "Hmm. And hot coffee!"

"Look, Hannah." Beth pointed out the open kitchen window, smiling widely. "You have a visitor."

Hannah came to stand by her. In between the flowering lavender and the blooming rhododendron, his back to the house as he looked out at the sea, stood Alex. On the patio table behind him was a tray with four steaming paper cups of coffee and a large paper bag from the bakery stand.

"When did he get here?" Sara asked, joining them at the window. "Hannah, let him in!"

"Yes. Yes, of course." Hannah hurried to unlock and throw open the kitchen door. "Alex! Alex!"

He turned around, his blue eyes smiling, his hands in the pockets of his jeans. "Hey, gorgeous," he said. "I was waiting for you."

"I was waiting for you too." Hannah stepped out and closed the door behind her, aware her friends were still at the window, rooting for her. "I'm finally home."

He came to her and brushed a curl behind her ear. "I owe you a breakfast, a dance, and a goodnight kiss," he murmured, taking her into his arms. "Which one do you want?"

"The kiss," she whispered, melting into his embrace, her skin tingling at his touch. "The dance later, when we're alone."

His lips met hers, tenderly at first, then deepening with a longing that mirrored her own. Their bodies fit together perfectly, the embrace a sweet promise of the love that had returned to her heart. As they pulled away, their eyes met again, speaking volumes without saying a word. In that moment, Hannah knew without a doubt that love had found its way back to her heart.

"Your friends are watching," he murmured, his hand trailing up her back in a tender caress. "Go have breakfast with them. I'll see you tonight. I'm not done kissing you, Hannah. I'll never be done."

All Hannah could do was nod, feeling the warmth of his touch and the overwhelming joy of their love that was as old and as new as the tide of the sea.

"I love you," he murmured and pressed a kiss in her hair.

"I love you too," Hannah whispered back.

"Mhm." With a low growl, Alex let her go and stepped back before sending a crooked smile at the kitchen window. "Ladies."

"Stay," Hannah said suddenly. "Don't leave again, Alex. I don't want just a taste and a trial, and I don't want half-hearted. I want all of you."

"You want all of me?" He lowered his head, searching her face with his starry gaze. "Are you sure?"

The distant sound of waves echoed the beat of her heart in a rhythm as timeless as the ocean itself. For the first time in a long while, Hannah felt truly at home. "Yes," she said and reached for his hand. "I'm sure."

Thank you for reading The Mendocino Book Club! To stay in beautiful Mendocino Beach and continue the story, read The Mendocino Beach House!

Mendocino Cove Series

"I loved it all, the history, the mystery, the sea, the love of family and friends...!"

Just over the bluff from Mendocino Beach lies the beautiful town of Mendocino Cove, home to its own feel-good series full of wonderful characters! Four friends are taking a second chance on love, life, and family as they start over together. Set among golden hills covered in wildflowers, vineyards brimming with sweet grapes, and a rugged coastline hiding secrets from the past, this series will keep you entertained until the last page.

BEACH COVE SERIES

"What an awesome series! Captivated in the first sentence! Beautiful writing!"

Maisie returns to charming Beach Cove and meets a heartwarming cast of old friends and new neighbors. The beaches are sandy and inviting, the sea is bluer than it should be, and the small town is brimming with big secrets. Together, Maisie and her sisters of the heart take turns helping each other through trials, mysteries, and matters of the heart. You can sign up for Nellie's newsletter to get a free prequel to the series!

BAY HARBOR BEACH SERIES

"Wonderfully written story. Rumors abound in this tale of loves and secrets."

Lose yourself in this riveting feel-good saga of old secrets and new beginnings. Best friends support each other through life's ups and downs and matters of the heart as they boil salt water taffy, browse quaint stores for swimsuits, and sample pies at the Beach Bistro!

ABOUT THE AUTHOR

Nellie Brooks writes feel-good friendship fiction for women. In her books you'll find flawed, likable characters who bake and adopt animals, gorgeous coastal settings that will make you study your tea leaves for the next vacation date, secrets that are best solved together, and happy endings until every estranged friend and distant sister is safe in the arms of her small town community.

Visit www.nelliebrooks.com or subscribe to her newsletter to learn about releases, promos, and writing news! You can also follow Nellie on Facebook and BookBub.

Made in the USA
Las Vegas, NV
08 October 2024

96509438R00146